CRIME AND TERROR IN THE JUNGLE

CRIME AND TERROR IN THE JUNGLE

VIRGINIA DE VOS

For John

ACKNOWLEDGEMENTS

I like to acknowledge the contribution of my two children Jeremy and Kim and their spouses for their support in my writing.

Rachel Rowlands from the United Kingdom for her assistance with a full manuscript review.

Dr Rohini Anandaraja for her support and encouragement.

Christine Anne Borra, Martin O'Connor and other staff at Your Books New Zealand in the publication of this novel.

Loris a wildlife magazine of Sri Lanka and other wildlife books on elephants.

PROLOGUE

Digby tossed and turned in the heat of the watch hut. He had the indelible image in his mind of a dead elephant lying at his feet, whilst he was stuck in the reeds in the water tank. A baby elephant was whimpering at his side, with the mother elephant charging towards him. His life flashed before his eyes, and he had moments to live. He grabbed his gun and fired but missed. Another shot rang out straight into the elephant's gaping mouth. She came down hard on her baby, took it in her trunk, stamped on it, and fell dead on her baby, crushing it to pulp.

This was a scene he conjured up in his mind repeatedly, in his waking hours, often in his nightmares. His Uncle Fred was asleep by his side, whilst they were awaiting the appearance of the poachers in the moonlight. It was now an all-out war against them. A do or die battle.

He remembered being a young seven-year-old boy, caring for and feeding his small baby elephant Raja, gifted to him by his grandparents' kind neighbour, who had numerous elephants on his large property, where the neighbour cared for Raja there. He would meet his pet daily whenever he visited his grandparents whilst on holidays from his Colombo school.

One night Raja disappeared; his grandma gave him the sad news. Digby cried for days after that, and never recovered from that loss. *'Now was the time to seek revenge,'* he told himself. The poachers had to be caught; the masterminds identified, and 'revenge was sweet,' was his slogan. They had to pay for stealing his pet baby elephant all those years ago.

Uncle Fred awoke hearing a rustle outside in the jungle, and together with Digby, stepped outside into the moonlight to investigate. Two elephants were breaking branches about two hundred metres away. The men had to be very quiet; elephants have acute hearing is what they reckoned. Getting back into their camp beds they tried to get back to sleep, but that was impossible with the lurking danger outside. Maybe the poachers would appear as well; this was an unseen enemy they were trying to overcome. The breaking of branches continued, and then a loud trumpeting. An elephant was disturbed, the poachers had to be around.

ONE

HUNTING A MAN EATER

It was an evil atmosphere tracking the hot and humid jungle of the East Coast of Vakarani in Sri Lanka. The ground was damp with rain-soaked leaves, decaying insects and moss. Digby Trott and his uncle Fred were on a hunt, commissioned by the Eastern Province Government Agent to gun-down the man-eating leopard which had recently sprung on an unsuspecting mail peon walking on a lonely country road, taking the mail from one small hamlet to the next. Digby, a twenty-three-year-old, with dark wavy hair and sharp features was a tall lean man, muscular from gym workouts and karate black belt skills.

'I thought I had a fleeting glimpse of a large leopard in the thick undergrowth and heard him snarl,' Digby whispered to Fred.

'Poachers too seem to be around,' Digby whispered to Fred. 'Their traps are everywhere.'

'There is evidence of a makeshift trap having been laid out here, but the rains have washed it away.'

'Those poachers are a menace,' Digby went on. 'Do you know

that when I was seven years old, I was gifted a baby elephant by a wealthy neighbour who had a few elephants as pets, when my grandparents were living in the Hill Country. I used to visit it daily when I went to their tea estate during my school holidays. It was kept on our neighbour's large property with its mother and a few other elephants. Some poachers managed to get into the compound, and they stole my pet. I was devastated and hate them immensely.'

Fred concurred with his nephew. 'Poachers are notoriously difficult to catch, they know all the tricks of avoiding detention. You will need plenty of help and expertise to apprehend them. Some good advice as well.'

'I will call on you if I need to. In the meantime, I will have to return to life in Gippsland, and back to earning a living.' Digby busied himself, getting his tent cleared, and packing his backpack.

That had put into his mind the seeds of vengeance for the criminals that walked the jungles doing harm to animals and the country. He was determined to fight their evil activities and try to reduce the carnage they inflicted on wildlife in the jungles around the world.

He slowly came down to earth from his 'adrenaline high,' planning to return to life at his parents' family farm in Gippsland, Victoria, Australia, ecstatic that he would witness the death of a notorious man-eater, having learnt some jungle habitats and shooting skills. Digby and Fred were commissioned to capture the man-eating leopard of Vakarani, and together with four labourers, were scouring the jungle around a water tank filled with recent rains. Mosquitoes and insects flying around them didn't deter Digby, donning gumboots to enter the inviting water to cool off in the sweltering heat.

Fred remained on the bank, with his shot gun slung over his

shoulder, looking around furtively into the jungle.

Suddenly there was a snarl and a growl, and an enormous leopard leapt out of the bushes, and headed straight for Digby, who froze. His legs were caught up in the reeds, and he felt all colour drain from his face.

Screaming out, 'Fred, where are you, I'm trapped here. Help me.' Digby lunged to a side just as a shot rang out, and Fred's accurate marksmanship hit the leopard straight at its heart. It dropped dead and fell into the water.

Digby trembling, muttering, 'I can't stop this trembling and the nausea I feel. My heart is beating so fast, I can hardly breathe. Let me lie down on the bank. That was mind-blowing. Death missed me by seconds.'

Fred came running, holding his chest and the shot gun in his arm, 'That was such a sly animal, cunning and cruel. The man-eater indeed, killing humans in numbers. We must get this gruesome beast back to the village.' He instructed the labourers to carry the animal on a pole back to their village.

Digby adding, 'Give me a few minutes to catch my breath. I'm a nervous wreck.'

The request from the Government Agent to kill the notorious animal was now completed. Stumbling around, Digby almost fell over a rotting corpse. 'For crying out loud, the sound of blue bottles buzzing around the half-eaten dead peon, makes it the stench of rotting eggs. This must have been the monster's last victim.'

Fred held his nose. 'I can't breathe with the stench. This poor guy needs a burial. Let's dig a trench, and put his body into it, with a mound on top.' He signalled to the labourers to start digging. Saying a prayer over the grave they moved on, going as fast as they could, as darkness descended over them.

Coming into the village they were surrounded by the entire crowd, eager to lay eyes on the hated animal. Devil dancers were summoned to cast out the evil spirit in the dead animal. They arrived with head and face masks on; two of them, bare bodied to the waist, with dhotis, began stomping on the ground in bare feet, chanting and going into a trance. There was a raucous celebration around a pit fire with much stomping of feet and dancing, all the villagers joining in with the devil dancers.

The leopard was later skinned and stuffed and put into a museum in Colombo, to forever remind people of the notorious man-eater.

TWO

TWO YEARS LATER

MORWELL GIPPSLAND

The alpacas and cattle vied with each other for their morning chew, whilst the guard dog circled around them, yapping at their hooves. The cool morning mist enveloped the nearby hills of the Trott family farm. Digby woke to the sounds of a kookaburra calling its mate, and he felt an inner tranquillity, as he drank in the sights and sounds of the bucolic world around him.

'Mum, Dad, I'll be meeting up with Scott today,' he called out.

'That's fine, but make sure you clean out your room first,' Gladys Trott called back.

'I could do with some help moving the cattle to the next paddock as well,' John called in from the shed. 'There's always work to be done around here, whilst you are off socialising.'

'What will you do once I leave for Melbourne now that I've got my degree?' A clearly irritated Digby walked up to the shed, to glower at his father. His calm mood had vanished instantly.

Visions of a strict and controlling father always just below his consciousness, of yelling matches and tears in childhood. Resentfully, he helped move the cattle, got into his car, and stormed off.

Scott's house was a half hour drive away; Digby needed to meet his close mate from his high school years. Scott Taylor, a six foot, twenty-five-year-old, with blonde hair and a stubby beard was relaxing at his parent's farmhouse.

'Whoa, what's the rush, I heard you rev your engine miles away!' Scott yelled at Digby above his engine roar.

'I wish my father would be more civil towards me; he hardly ever talks kindly, maybe you could instil some tactful talk into him.' Digby was trying anything he could to change his father.

Scott nodded but didn't really want to interfere in Digby's family arguments.

'I must fill you in with my jungle adventures, even though I know it isn't your "cup of tea," plus, I must find a job in IT and somewhere to live in Melbourne, maybe we could go down together soon. I understand you too will be looking for work in Aircraft Engineering somewhere local.'

'Yes, that's true. We can go down together on Monday to scout around the city fringe; a one-bedroom apartment should do you fine.'

'Scotty, I hope your friend can accommodate us while we are in Melbourne. I have a deep hatred of all animal poachers and will bore you to death when I regale you with my jungle titbits.'

'Can't wait!' Scott said lazily.

'Nevertheless, I must tell you that I have a super marksman in my uncle Fred, who killed a man-eating leopard in the Sri Lankan jungles a couple of years ago, when I joined him on the hunt of a lifetime. That's one for the record books.'

The two mates walked down to the local pub for a quiet drink and a chat, something they tried to do as often as they could, but which would become rarer as they both secured jobs.

•••

'I must organise accommodation in Melbourne soon. Let's go down there on Monday.'

The following Monday they drove down in Digby's car to stay with a friend of Scott's and scour the real estate agents' offices for accommodation. The rental market in Melbourne around the central business district was booming, and it was easy enough securing a suitable apartment in the city. They located a one-bedroom, small apartment, which needed basic furniture. Scott and he organised the loan of a bed, a couch, a small dining table with chairs, a fridge, and kitchen utensils: just adequate for his needs. The utility services had to be connected and the bond paid, making a loan from his parents necessary, much to Digby's chagrin. They returned to his parents' home, to collect crockery and cutlery, linen, and other essentials for his newfound independence.

'Scott, I must now apply for a job, and do it soon. I'm seriously short of cash.'

Returning to Morwell, to scour the internet for work, he sent off a couple of applications, and Digby waited. It wasn't long before he was employed and moved out of home, much to the delight of his father, but not his mother. John always thought Digby was a 'mama's boy' and overindulged him with too much attention, of which John was resentful.

Digby's small apartment overlooked the city. It was sparse with its bits of borrowed furniture. He remarked to Scott, 'I'll have to learn to do some basic cooking, and cleaning. Not my pet chores.

I'll also enrol in a gym around the corner, that should be fun, together with continuing my karate classes.'

Thus, life went on for a few weeks while Digby tried to settle into city life; a man from the bush who wanted to live in the country, but of necessity needed to live in the city.

•••

At seven pm on a cold winter's Friday night in Melbourne, Digby was walking home from the gym after work, when he decided to take a short cut home through a darkened, quiet alleyway. The night air smelt of evil and sent shivers down Digby's spine. Something didn't seem right, but he tried to brush it aside as his fantasy. He had a sixth sense he was being stalked. After a while he heard footsteps, several of them, and realised he was being followed. He increased his walk to a jog, and the footsteps increased. Then, suddenly, he felt an almighty whack to the back of his head. This twenty-five-year-old saw stars, he was terrified.

'What the fricking hell, you hooligans,' he screamed, 'get off me!'

He moved his arms trying to block their punches, and used his legs the best way he could, to cut them off. He was sweating, and felt blood trickling into his mouth, from a head wound. No time to think, he had to run; he knew there were two of them, wearing hoodies, and long trousers. Stumbling, he found his way into a well-lit street. They were after his phone and his wallet, he surmised; and disappeared as soon as car headlights were on them. Trembling, shaking, and weak, he staggered along to his apartment lift. Fumbling he opened his door and fell inside on his couch.

Bleeding, aching all over, he reached for his phone, and dialled 'triple 0.'

'Fire, Ambulance or Police?' the operator enquired.

'P-p-police,' he spat out the word.

'Sargent Yates from Melbourne Police,' a gruff voice came over.

'I have just been attacked in the city, in a narrow alleyway, by two young hooligans.'

'Can you describe them?'

'Not very well.'

'Give me your address and a patrol car will be over shortly.'

Putting an ice pack onto his head wound, he tried to stop the bleeding; then he poured himself a scotch, and tried to settle down on his couch, waiting for the police to arrive. When they did, he was quizzed,

'Can you describe them?'

'Two young Caucasians, agitated, about twenty to twenty-two years old, in dark pants and hoodies. Maybe they were drug fuelled.' He tried to understand what had just happened.

'Very well, we'll be in touch, and may need to speak to you again.'

He then phoned Scott.

'Digby you sound terrible, why are you calling me at this ungodly hour? It's one am.'

'I've been mugged in the city whilst returning from the gym. I'm aching all over my body. I'm bleeding from a head wound and have a whopping headache.'

'Hang in there. I'll be over as soon as I can. You need to see a doctor in the morning. Who knows you may have a broken bone or two?'

Scott, an outgoing friendly man was Digby's prop, an old friend he could always rely on, so he told himself. They had played football together for the Traralgon Tigers, flew model aeroplanes, and were due to work weekends crop dusting in light planes out of the local airport.

Scott arrived at Digby's home at daybreak.

'What the hell is the matter with city life? I hate it. This is the initiation I get just after I arrive. I would like to return to the quiet, peaceful county life,' Digby was ranting on.

'Calm down mate, every city has its drawbacks. You'll soon become accustomed to the crime, and learn to avoid it, if you can. We must get you down to a doctor to check you out.' Scott drove his mate down to the local doctor's surgery and Digby was glad to get cleared of any broken bones. He had suffered just cuts and bruises. He had them seen to and soon looked like the walking wounded.

'I am just settling into my new job, which is rather mundane now, but I guess it will pick up as I go along.'

Scott added, 'I concur with you. My job in aeronautical engineering is complicated and I must get accustomed to the ins and outs of it, but I'm loving it.'

Scott stayed the weekend at his mate's place tending to his needs and generally being both a mother and father to him helping him tune into city life, the little that Scott knew of it.

THREE

A CHANCE MEETING

Two weeks later Digby decided to go down to the local Dragon Arms Pub on a Friday evening to unwind after work. It was crowded with the aroma of sweat, cigarette smoke and loud voices filling the air. Digby was diffident, and trying to be unobtrusive, he found himself a quiet spot at the bar and ordered a beer. The barman and bar-lady were busy, but not too busy to chat.

'You new here?' asked the barman. 'Haven't seen you around,' whilst pouring drinks for the men at the bar, trying to engage with as many customers as he could.

'As a matter of fact, I am. Have just relocated from the bush and am beginning to get a feel of the big smoke.'

'Do you like it here?'

'Talk to me in a couple of months.' Digby looked around to find a vacant seat in the crowded smoke-filled room.

A long-legged twenty-four-year-old blonde woman came across from a nearby table and sat next to Digby, greeting him. A beautiful woman with perfect makeup, covering a beautiful face, piercing blue eyes, gold round earrings, wearing a loose blue blouse and knee length blue tight skirt. She sat next to him, oozing perfume. Digby looked at her in amazement. This was something he could get used to. He was transfixed, admiring every facet of her face, neck and upper body. For a minute he couldn't believe his eyes that such a beautiful woman would want to sit next to him. Up until now he had human contact only with work and gym acquaintances. He was trying to focus his recently battered head and eyes on her after his recent melee, not being too successful. He held out his hand to her.

'I'm Digby Trott.'

She reciprocated, 'I'm Zelma Evans. New here?'

'As a matter of fact, I am. Just relocated from South Gippsland and have started work here recently. Don't know much about Melbourne. Can I buy you a drink?'

'Vodka for me, thanks. I'll have to give you a "Cook's tour" of Melbourne sometime.' Zelma was trying to shout above the noise in the bar.

'It's too stuffy and noisy in here. Let's move outside into some clean air,' Digby suggested. He was nervous, had sweaty palms and mild hand tremors but tried not to show it. Outside they would be able to see and talk to each other better, is what Digby reckoned. Finding a quiet table and chairs, they sat trying to make small talk; he aware of the awkwardness of his conversation. After a while he suggested, 'I live quite close by, why don't we move to my place, or maybe tee up an evening at a local restaurant?' Zelma warmly welcomed the idea. With that they exchanged phone numbers and addresses, agreeing to meet the next evening, and they walked out together.

•••

Digby arrived at Zelma's apartment on Saturday evening, when she greeted him at her door. She liked what she saw, Digby dressed casually in open necked shirt, jeans and jacket. His hair tousled, wearing a woody men's fragrance, and well-polished shoes. 'Hello, handsome,' she greeted him warmly. He reciprocated with a light kiss on her face, and admired the woman he saw, her hair set in a bun and gold earrings, with her trademark stiletto heels, and a well-fitting dress. She stood just a few inches shorter, and noticed that he was left-handed, making her think he must be creative or intelligent or both.

'I have booked a table at the Cuckoo Restaurant by the sea,' she added.

They left in Digby's car for the suburb of Williamstown. It was a cool summer evening, the sea looked as calm as a pond from the second-floor dining room, where the evening sun was going down slowly throwing copper and red across a blue sky. They ordered drinks and canapes before dinner. A delightful sea food meal was on the menu.

'So, what do you do for work?' Zelma tentatively asked, adding, 'I work as a secretary to the manager of a white goods company in the city.'

'I've just started work as an IT Consultant for a big company, in the city as well, having recently graduated from university. I also fly light planes out of Traralgon airport on some weekends, having done a light plane pilot's course.' Digby went on, not wanting to sound pompous. 'It's more of a hobby job, really…'

'That's interesting. I'll have to show you around Melbourne, the tennis centre, the museums, the Arts Centre, the Eureka Tower and maybe the Botanical Gardens. There's just so much to see and experience in Melbourne, not to mention the night life and theatrical shows,' she said, delighting at the idea of showing a good-looking man around the city.

After dinner Zelma started feeling hot and sweaty and began to hyperventilate. She started shaking, and became nauseous. She said, 'I feel the room spinning around,' excusing herself, and she rushed off to the Ladies room. She returned looking pale, flushed in her face, and short of breath. 'This is so embarrassing, and on our first date too.'

Digby wasn't quite sure what the problem was, all he knew was that he had to get Zelma home. He settled the bill and helped her to his car.

'I sometimes get these panic attacks, which often come out of the blue, and I usually keep a brown paper bag to breathe into but forgot to bring it with me tonight. I feel embarrassed at ruining your night out.'

'Not at all. Let's get you home and into bed. Let me know how you are tomorrow and maybe a drive into the country could be the perfect tonic.'

•••

The next day being Sunday they both took it easy, Digby collecting Zelma from her apartment at mid-morning. They planned a leisurely drive out of Melbourne heading towards Geelong, taking the seaside road, and stopping for coffee along the way. Driving, Digby went on, 'I guess I need to fill you in on myself,' Digby declared. 'I was born in Sri Lanka to an Aussie father and a Burgher mother, which means she's of European descent. I spent my early years in Colombo, where my father was employed by a British company, and where I went to primary school. My mum's parents lived on a tea estate in the hill country, and we often joined them on trips to the wildlife sanctuaries of Yala and Wilpattu, where I was introduced to elephant, leopard and sloth bear, as well as deer, crocodile and other smaller wildlife. I loved those trips, and guess I learnt about animals in the wild. My father's parents ran a farm in Gippsland, and that's where I had my secondary education, as my parents co-managed the farm with my grandparents. I also hate poachers, as they are responsible for stealing my pet baby elephant, a pet that was gifted to me when I was seven years old. But that's another story and I don't want to regale you with all that detail today.'

Zelma listened wide eyed. 'My goodness, that's quite a story. I'm afraid mine is quite boring and staid.'

Digby went on, 'I have a close friend Scott Taylor, twenty-five years old, from Morwell. We went to High School together. Being an only child, he is like a brother to me, which is how I see him, anyway. You will meet him sooner or later.'

They stopped at a small cafe for lunch, followed by a quiet walk on the seashore. Digby put his arm around Zelma, and she snuggled up close to him. Finding a seat, they relaxed for a while, before heading back to his car, and the drive back home. Returning to his apartment, on the top floor of the apartment complex, Zelma was rather taken aback to see the mess it was in. Clothes strewn all over the room, bed hastily made, stale coffee cup on his bedside table. The wall had a picture of a large leopard drinking water at a dam, with a green rug thrown over the couch. The fridge door didn't shut easily, and the television needed a bang on the top to start it. Dust was all over the tables. The dining table was a small round table with a laminate finish. Zelma told herself, 'This is a bachelor pad if ever there was one. He will need some housekeeping lessons.'

'I must apologise for the state of this apartment; I'm not very good at housekeeping as you can see. Let's just sit and relax, we can get a take out for dinner.' Digby had intended to clean up in a day or two, and had to admit her visit was a bit of a surprise.

Turning on his stereo they danced to some romantic music he played. Sitting down they kissed passionately, and he felt hot in the groin, but decided it was too early for any sex, which Zelma was happy to go along with. Cuddling on the sofa listening to a singer crooning on his stereo, whilst having a drink to relax, was all they needed for the present.

•••

The next Friday Digby and Zelma had planned a dinner for seven pm, when at six thirty pm he received a phone call from Scott.

'Digby, there's been a fire at the Traffic Control Tower at Traralgon Airport and all pilots are asked to attend to help with its control.'

'My goodness, Scotty, I have a dinner date with Zelma, and hate to stand her up. But I'll be there as soon as I can, it's a two-hour drive.' Digby was clearly frustrated at having to cancel his date.

'Darling, I'm so sorry, Scott has just called me to attend a fire at Traralgon Airport, and I must rush down there. I promise to make it up to you.'

'Digby, I was so looking forward to our dinner tonight. I understand and will hopefully see you on Sunday.'

He rushed off to get on the Princes Highway and headed to Traralgon. Arriving there he saw the fire from miles away, there was complete mayhem, with fire trucks everywhere, and firemen with hoses trying to extinguish the fire in the Controller's Tower. Scott came up to him, saying he got the impression it was the work of an arsonist, but the aeroplanes were all safe. The two of them joined in, trying to help wherever they could, and it was midnight before they got to Scott's apartment, exhausted, poured themselves a stiff whisky each, and got into their beds for the night.

•••

On Saturday morning they returned to the airport to view the charred remains of the surrounding vegetation and runway and noticed an unkempt looking man around thirty years of age, loitering around the place, even though it was a crime scene.

Scott walked up to him, 'Mate, what are you doing here?'

'I saw the flames go up last night, and thought I'd come down and have a look,' the man said, shifting from foot to foot.

'Oh, is that so. What's your name?' added Digby.

'Jack Smith. I live on the outskirts of Morwell.' He was a skinny man of average height, with wispy shoulder length hair, a toothy grin, wearing a shabby shirt and shorts, obviously in need of a good bath, and with evidence of slowness of mind.

'Oh yes,' Digby added, 'do you live close enough to have seen what was going on?'

'There were a couple of planes landing, and then all of a sudden there was a loud bang, with smoke and flames everywhere.' Jack had a faraway look in his eyes, not looking straight at Scott and Digby, giving the impression he may not have been truthful.

'Well, we would like to know more. Why don't we go past your place in Morwell, and then have lunch at the Morwell Hotel?' Digby said nonchalantly.

'What do I get out of all this? Are you two a couple of coppers investigating?'

'Here's fifty dollars to help you with any financial difficulties. That, mind you, is not to be sniffed at. We are not the police,' Scott chirpily added.

'Alright, let's go,' said Jack, grabbing the money.

They got into Scott's car, the smell of stale perspiration, unwashed clothes, and cigarette smoke was nauseating. All windows lowered, they drove past Jack's tiny one bedroom weather-board miner's cottage with overgrown lawn, on a dirt road, ten minutes out of town. It was run down with a water tank in the back yard, and the sound of barking dogs. A sturdy wire fence ran around the garden, giving space for his numerous dogs to run around. Empty beer cans and beer bottles were strewn everywhere.

'This is my home left to me by an old aunt. I can barely pay the rates and feed my three dogs when I am unemployed, but when I'm lucky I get labouring jobs in town. I have a bicycle I use to get around. I've been trying to get a steady job, doing any type of work, but have not had much luck,' said Jack displaying a nervous facial tic.

'What about your family?' Digby ventured tentatively.

'Well, my father was a villain. He would keep me home from getting to school on time, which landed me in trouble, and punished with after-school detention. He was always drunk and beat me up for no reason. I hated him.'

They drove onto the Morwell Hotel and ordered from the a la carte menu. Keen to obtain more information, they kept asking Jack more questions.

'I'm sure you two are f…ing coppers, asking all these questions. It's none of your business anyway.'

'Okay mate, here's another fifty dollars to help you.' Scott came to the rescue.

'My poor mother tried to stand up to him, but she got beaten up as well, so we lived with my mother's sister who had no children, and when Mum died and later her sister died, I had nowhere to go. I was fifteen when Aunt Betty took me to live with her. I have one older sister, three years older than I am, but she was adopted out when young, and I have no contact with her.'

'What were you like at school?' asked Digby.

'Not too brilliant,' said Jack nervously, tapping his fingers on the table. 'Had to repeat a couple of year levels at High School.'

'What about after leaving school?'

'Not much to boast about, I guess. I had a few run ins with the coppers, just as I was getting to look after myself, was in the juvenile court for shoplifting, breaking and entering, and fire setting.'

'Fire setting!' said Digby and Scott in unison, exchanging glances; both presumed Jack had a drinking problem, and a shady past. He was the classic unstable drifter and odd personality. It must have been the only decent meal he'd had in days, and they were somehow drawn to this unfortunate man, for no reason, other than sympathy.

'No that's not correct. My mistake,' Jack interjected and clamped up refusing to give out any more personal information.

After lunch they parted ways, having obtained Jack's Aunt Betty's phone number, as Jack didn't own a phone. Digby and Scott had now become vigilantes, trying to determine if Jack was the fire setter at the Traralgon Airport. They both thought Jack was the prime suspect, but the police had to reinforce that belief, and they were not aware of how far the police investigations had moved along. They returned to Scott's place, with a plan for Scott to follow up on Jack, and Digby was to return to Melbourne.

FOUR

THREE MONTHS LATER

Digby and Zelma were now an item. They enjoyed each other's company and shared several mutual interests. Digby was keen for Zelma to get to know his folks.

'Zelma, my love, I think it's time you met my parents. Why don't we go to their farm this weekend, as well as get a feel for country life? I'm sure you will learn to like it.'

Zelma agreed, and they set out on Friday after work, taking the highway to Gippsland and Morwell. It was exhilarating to both, driving past farms with calm cattle grazing peacefully, or sheep wandering around large green pastures. An avenue of conifers looked majestic beside the highway. Digby always felt a sense of peace leaving the city behind, inhaling clean country air. After a two-hour drive, they reached the Trott family small acreage farm. Gladys and John were mustering the cattle into another paddock, and Digby jumped out of the car to assist them.

Gladys met them, cheerily welcoming them both. 'Zelma, my dear, we are so glad to meet you, having heard so much about you.'

John added, 'Digby seems better since he has met you, he doesn't fly off into rages with me especially. That's a good thing, for him and for me.'

'Oh, is that so, Dad. I must say it "takes two to tango," you are no saint yourself if I may say so.'

'Do come into our humble abode, I've got dinner ready.' Gladys was welcoming.

The smell of a farmhouse was something new to Zelma; cow poo smell in the garden, mud marks on the floorboards at the entrance, chickens running around, rather untidy inside the house, whilst the guest room they would use was spotless. There was plenty of bird life around, kookaburras, lorikeets, rosellas, fairy wrens, galahs, cockatoos, parrots and wild duck.

Zelma whispered to Digby when alone, 'Your parents seem delightful. Your mum obviously thinks you are the "apple of her eye." I'm going to have a bit of competition! It will be a learning experience for me to walk around the farm and see how it's run.'

Dinner was a simple casserole meal with freshly baked bread, and fresh fruit for dessert.

The next morning Gladys had made scones and flapjacks for breakfast, with homemade jam, which delighted Zelma. 'These taste yummy. nothing like fresh country air to work up an appetite,' she whispered to Digby.

After breakfast they walked around to the milking shed, in gumboots, Zelma careful to tread lightly.

'Look, look there's a baby calf, must be a few days old! How delightful. Perhaps I can try my hand at milking,' Zelma exclaimed, and tried to milk an irritable cow, much to Digby's delight, but that effort didn't last long to an irritable cow. So, they wandered past cattle, an excited sheep dog, and dodged a fox scurrying away.

'Let's have a look at the dam, there's plenty of water in it after all the rains. Gladys says it is a man-made dam,' Zelma enthused.

To which Digby added, 'Yes, there wasn't a single dam here when they moved in.'

The farmer in the adjoining farm had planted snow peas and was trying to scare away the pesky crows trying to peck his emerging crop, by firing a rifle in the air. He gave them a cheery wave.

The long walk around made them both tired and hungry ending up in their beds for a siesta.

That evening John and Gladys took the young couple around town to show Zelma something of what rural life was all about.

'There's a musical show going on tonight, I'd love to watch them perform. Country singers and a mini contest will make my day,' an enthusiastic Zelma said to the others, who all nodded in agreement. Country music performed by local musicians vying for a trophy brought out some undiscovered talent; the day ending with a glorious fireworks display.

•••

The next morning the wind sighed through the pine trees, and the rising sun coloured the mist as it rolled down the green hills, to rise again lifting from the valley. The clouds in the distance sped across the sky, copper and red against the milky blue. Digby yawned and stretched sitting on the veranda, with Zelma sipping a cup of coffee.

'There's a Swap Meet on in town today, with horse jumping, an Australian drover's dog showing how to rally six sheep into a wooden enclosure, and plenty of goods to buy and sell. I think we should go down and have a look,' Digby informed Zelma.

John, happened to overhear this, and remarked, 'Digby, maybe you could give me a hand with fixing a part of the broken wire fence.'

'Dad, you know I am no good at that type of handyman work. I've got plans to take Zelma around. Don't bug me to be your handyman, I know labour in the country is scarce, but this is my time. Maybe I'll have a look when we return.'

Zelma felt embarrassed for Digby, at this encounter, leaving Gladys once more, to calm things down.

After breakfast Digby and Zelma left for the town to enjoy the Swap Meet and the shows, with a horse rally and a farm dog display on the agenda. Several tents were pitched, and inside each tent were typical country wares, home-made jams and pickles, honey, plants by the dozen, and hand knitted woollies. The happy sound of a brass band added to the festive atmosphere, while country folk walked around with smiles and cheery words, greeting each other happily. There was a real community atmosphere; the weather being bright and sunny as well.

'I just wish my father would stop getting under my skin when I visit, he needs to drink less, then maybe he won't have such a short fuse. When is he ever going to learn to respect my lifestyle? I'm not his sidekick,' Digby whispered to Zelma.

The show was a good introduction to country life for Zelma, she was slowly coming round to what Digby hoped would be a love of the rural lifestyle.

Getting into Digby's car to return home, both feeling the love, a rejuvenated Digby asked Zelma, 'Hope you had an enjoyable trip. I must apologise on behalf of my father, at his unsociable behaviour.'

'I understand perfectly. Fathers sometimes can be difficult. Wait till you meet my father. He's no saint.'

'Mum was raised on a tea estate in the hill country of Sri Lanka, and Dad was raised on a farm here in Morwell, yet, he isn't the calm type, he was meant to be, as so many rural folks are. He flies off the handle so fast, maybe that's where I get it from!' an embarrassed Digby was trying to justify his father's behaviour. Zelma was trying to understand the relationship between father and son, and not quite getting there. She had to be super tactful, she told herself.

Having had a very relaxing and insightful weekend for Zelma especially, they drove back to Melbourne on Sunday afternoon. Driving into the setting sun was blinding, and Digby had to be careful to watch the road. Zelma often had to navigate and be a second pair of eyes. They arrived back after the ninety-minute drive, tired but happy.

•••

The following weekend, on the Saturday, being a rainy Melbourne day, they sat in Zelma's apartment. There was a moaning of thunder in the distance, and one by one fell the first drops of rain, which felt like the tears of the gods. They ordered a takeout and settled in for a cosy chat on the couch, by the fireplace.

'Zelma, you know how I love the rural life, just driving into the hills lifts my spirits. I was thinking of buying a small shack to get to on the weekends. Why don't we go down one weekend and see what's on the market?'

'Yes, but what are you saying, Digby? Are you telling me you want to live in the outback? I'm not the country type, you know that. Where will that leave me? I'm not sure I'll want to go down to Gippsland, or wherever you fancy, every weekend. There's so much to do here in Melbourne, you'll feel the vibe with time, I assure you. I will give your idea some thought. I do love the Melbourne life, the theatre, football matches, the museums, the arts, it's endless.'

'No worries, take your time. It's only for the occasional weekend. It'll be worth it, I guarantee.'

Trying to steer Digby away from something she was unhappy talking about, Zelma felt she needed to distract him away from his newfound preoccupation. This was something she found hard to digest. Small country towns were not her scene.

'Perhaps I might tell you something of my parents. Dad was a travelling salesman for a soft drink company, and away from home for long periods. Mum was always stressed having to care for us girls on her own. She was extremely strict with me, I guess, being the eldest, I was supposed to be the responsible one. To get her attention and affection I had to submit to her rules, and there were so many, but I really wanted her to hug and kiss me. I had to help her in so many ways, and if I didn't, she would threaten me with the naughty corner or report me to Dad. I loved my dad and wished he had been home more often.'

'Oh, you poor thing, that must have been awful for you. I can't imagine your predicament. Let's make things better now!'

Zelma started perspiring, and breathing rapidly, saying she felt nauseous. She looked pale and had Digby worried.

'I feel another panic attack coming on. I'll just take a tablet, that should fix it. I do apologise,' Zelma said grabbing a brown paper bag. She rushed into a bedroom and breathed into the bag, four breaths at a time. Then she lay down to get rid of her headache.

Digby thought that perhaps unhappy memories hadn't helped. He covered her with a doona in bed and just lay down on the couch for a while, falling asleep in no time. The next day they were both re-energised, and feeling good, Zelma very apologetic for her panic attack, Digby just beginning to understand her plight.

•••

'I would like to introduce you to my family; perhaps we could go over this weekend.' Zelma wanted Digby to meet her family, now that they were an item, with a mutual love of the outdoors, and securing a social network. 'I love the newer man I see in you, not flying off the handle at minor everyday occurrences.'

'I'll take the compliment, thanks.'

'My mum's name is Joan, and my dad, David. My younger sisters are Ruth, two years my junior, and Denise five years younger than myself. Dad is now based in Melbourne; you will have to come and meet them. I'll fix a time for Saturday perhaps.'

They fixed a casual afternoon when cake and tea was lined up. She gave Digby a bit of a heads up on them. 'Mum was rather the nervous type, didn't like mixing with people she didn't know. Dad's social functions were often anathema to her, when I was in primary school. She improved as we girls got older. I love her dearly, and she was a good mother. She was more settled when dad didn't have to travel for work.'

On the Saturday they arrived at a neat brick house, in suburbia. Joan opened the door with a cheery smile, being a well-proportioned lady, motherly looking, dressed in a floral dress, her hair tied up in a bun.

'Hello Zelma and Digby, do come in. It's a pleasure to meet you, Digby,' and greeted them both with an affectionate kiss.

Ruth was sulking in her bedroom and refused to come out to meet them, and Denise was out collecting some groceries. David came out looking fit and well, from daily fitness runs, and with a firm handshake, greeted Digby.

'Hello, young man. I'm glad to meet you. Zelma seems over the moon with you!'

'Dad! No necessity for intricate details.'

Denise, rather plain looking compared to Zelma, arrived, saying, 'Is Ruth being anti-social again?'

Ruth retorted, 'Mind your own business, I'll do as I want.'

David tried to intervene, asking Digby, 'I understand you're a wildlife enthusiast and conservationist? Any good stories for us?'

Zelma sensed Digby's unease, adding, 'Dad, I'm sure Digby would like to fill you in with tales of his adventures, but not today.'

Ruth eventually came out. She was evidently the tomboy of the family. Dressed in boyish fashion in shorts and tee shirt, and a short haircut, she sat sulking. Zelma suggested they go into the garden and admire Joan's gardening skills, and Digby happily accepting. Joan had a beautiful garden with numerous rose bushes and other flowering plants that Zelma couldn't name. The potted anthuriums, however, were the showpiece of the family and took pride of place on the veranda. Joan had prepared cake and coffee, which brought the family together inside again. Ruth returned to her room, Denise sat down to play the piano and entertain them, clearly musical.

'Let's have a singsong: anyone wants to exercise their vocal cords?' Joan suggested, but it was met with a stony silence. Continuing with small talk about the weather and other mundane issues and feeling Digby's unease in the atmosphere of her family, after an hour's stay the young couple left, Joan throwing open an invitation for a meal, when they could fit it into their busy schedule.

'So, what did you think of my family?' Zelma asked on the drive back home.

'I liked them. Not having any siblings, I must say I saw a different side to family life. Ruth seems interesting! My family life was quiet, so I guess I had to argue with my father. I had no one to throw the salt at!'

•••

The following Saturday they planned to set off for Gippsland to look at properties for a weekender.

'There's a two-bedroom mud brick cottage in Mirboo North, on three acres of land, with wood-fire heating, and cooking on a wood-fire stove,' Digby enthused. Zelma reluctantly agreed to go down to have a look at.

Digby gave her a passionate kiss of approval, as they sat on his couch in tender embrace.

'I do appreciate you coming in on this plan, my love, it means a lot to me.'

Saturday was a clear sunny day when they left Melbourne for the highway, a ninety-minute drive to the township of Mirboo North in South Gippsland. Digby drank in the sights and sounds of the bucolic world around him, of the rolling green hills and mist covered mountains, and instantly felt relaxed. Calm and serene cattle grazing on the grass in one paddock, with sheep grazing in another. The clouds sped across the sky red and white and grey against the milky blue. The wide-open spaces and the conifers lining the highway like the forest of life, were relaxing to them both.

'Let's stop for coffee in Korumburra, a little country town with a wild west feel about it. There's only one supermarket in town, with a few souvenir shops along the main street, and the ever-necessary pubs; two of them. The locals are friendly and hospitable. It's about twenty minutes' drive from there to Mirboo.'

Zelma was fascinated; 'I do believe a horse and carriage is taking tourists for a drive. What a delight,' when she saw a horse and carriage being driven along a side dirt road. There were the pubs, a very essential football ground, present in every country town, a few churches and several miners' cottages from a by-gone era. There were even a couple of horses and their riders cantering along a side road, introducing Zelma to a different lifestyle. They decided a longer stay at another time was a proposition.

•••

'Now it's onto the Strzelecki Highway, and an even smaller town, Mirboo North to view the cottage I have in mind.' Scott was in attendance as well to give his opinion on the house, although Zelma was not too much in favour of what she called an intrusion into their time together. She made a mental note to tell Digby her views on this, when the time was right, not wanting to upset him when he was clearly happy with the small mud brick cottage which impressed him instantly.

'I love the views, the distant hills, the highway in the distance, and even the sea can be seen on a clear day.' Digby was clearly excited at what he saw whilst walking around the garden and then climbing the steps into the house.

'I'm not sure I can survive the loneliness, even as a weekender, and what I can see as an antediluvian and old- fashioned lifestyle,' Zelma voiced her thoughts out loud. 'And the garden is overgrown, I'm not one for gardening.' Digby raised his eyebrows at her vocabulary.

'Give it time, my love. Gardening is my forte, and in small rural towns there are plenty of young schoolboys looking for some extra pocket money. We can make it work.'

They wandered down the road to be greeted by the friendly farmer, getting his tractor all organised for planting snow peas in the adjoining paddock; with his stout mate, a large Labrador retriever, seated by his side. A kookaburra let out a shrill call to its mate; they were in rural heaven. A pub lunch at the local hotel was necessary to satisfy the hunger pangs of clean country air.

The return trip to Melbourne was a quiet one, each with their own thoughts.

Dropping Zelma off at her apartment, he stepped inside, for a short while because Zelma was keen to clear the air. 'I really did enjoy the trip today. Thank you. It showed me something of rural life.' Digby gave her a warm embrace in acknowledgement. 'I wasn't trying to rain on your parade...'

Digby skipped along leaving her apartment; he was happy.

The next move was to go through the formalities of securing a loan and putting in a tentative offer towards purchasing the cottage in Mirboo North, which took a few weeks to be decided on by the vendor who considered the offer too low. Digby then considered looking at other properties with Zelma gradually coming round to the idea of occasional visits to the country. He found property hunting too onerous, so raised his offer a miniscule, and considering the vendor desperately wanted to sell, the deal was sealed. Digby now had a place of his own, a short drive from Melbourne, whilst working at the Traralgon Airport on some weekends.

FIVE

AN APPLICATION IS MADE

Life was idyllic, but Digby was restless. He was a regular contributor to the Sri Lankan wildlife magazine the *Mynah*, and one publication ran an advertisement for an Elephant Conservationist to assist the Wildlife Department eliminate lawless poachers suspected of shooting or poisoning elephants whose numbers were dwindling: as well as the killing of leopard, deer, the jungle cat and other small animals.

The work was mainly in the Game Sanctuaries of Yala, Wilpattu and Gal Oya National Parks; two parks being near the coast, and the third inland. It was a short-term contract of a few weeks, being open ended. The Wildlife Conservation Society of America would provide financial assistance, and it was hoped the project wouldn't be longer than three months. The money offered was not all that enticing, but Digby wanted the thrill of adventure rather than the financial gain. The application had to be made to Mr Tissa Fernando, the manager of the Wildlife Department in Colombo.

Digby remembering his deep-seated hatred of poachers, and his experience assisting Fred, killing the man-eating leopard, decided to submit his application.

His mind was racing with all that this contract envisaged: adventure, detective investigation, the return to the jungle, and of course, the danger involved in confronting criminals, and his mind boggled. There were a few people he had to discuss this with: his parents to overlook his weekender; his boss regarding obtaining leave; Scott to cover for his piloting; and most importantly, Zelma.

He called his parents. 'Dad. I am contemplating applying for an overseas elephant conservation project leader to apprehend poachers in the Sri Lankan jungles, commencing in a couple of months. I feel suited to make this application having gained some confidence from my jungle trip with Uncle Fred.'

'Attempting to apprehend poachers who are killing wildlife for their tusks and their skins or bush meat is a noble task, but beware, these men are criminals and will stop at nothing if anyone should get in their way.'

Gladys who had heard the conversation on speaker phone added, 'Son, you were always one for adventure and risk taking, so please think carefully as to whether you want to do this, and make sure you have all the necessary information before you submit your application.'

Digby was acutely aware of his parents' angst and tried to placate them.

'I will take all your concerns on board, and get as much information as I can, presuming, of course, that I get the position.'

Scott was an easy person to convince. 'Sure, buddy, I'll cover for you, if this is what you really want to do. Keep me informed.'

Zelma may not be as easy as the others. It would have to be done over a weekend, Digby mused.

She already had to be convinced that a rural weekender was what he wanted to do, and now he was contemplating going overseas on a dangerous mission. He would need a good excuse to make her believe in him, and most importantly stay with him; he didn't want to lose her now. There was work to be done.

•••

Digby returned to Melbourne after a weekend of crop dusting. That night he had a dream.

He was visiting the Colombo Zoological Gardens with his parents when he was nine years old, seeing elephants performing in a circular arena. They moved to the beat of drums, had bells attached to their feet, and he marvelled at the magnificent creatures. During waking hours, he would reminisce on a wild elephant trumpeting loudly, and chasing their vehicle on an occasion when he visited the Yala Game Park. Could this be an omen, he wondered.

The following Friday he and Zelma set off for his holiday cottage, planning a quiet weekend. Waking the next morning they sat on the deck, with the green hills enveloped in mist and not visible at all. Trucks and cars were meandering on the highway in the distance. A kookaburra's call to its mate broke the silence, and soon there was an answer to his call. The small bird bath in the garden was overcrowded with tiny house sparrows, as well as rosellas, and galahs clambering for space, and making an awful noise. Sipping coffee, they watched as a lone kangaroo came bouncing out of nowhere to run among the cows in the next paddock. A lone fox followed him; the cows didn't tolerate this invasion, giving chase to the intruders. Digby's house sat on a hill, overlooking farmland, a torrent of green pasture that plummeted into a valley of fog and mist. Then as the mist cleared, the hills were visible again.

'Zelma, there is something I want to tell you.'

She sat upright. 'Yes, my love, I hope it's not bad news, you sound serious....'

'You know how I told you that I had spent my primary school years in Sri Lanka? Well, there is a position advertised for an Elephant Conservationist to take a team into the jungles there to apprehend poachers who are plundering their elephants and other wildlife. I intend applying for the position.'

Zelma sat in silence looking at him. She was stunned; she couldn't believe her ears.

'What is going to happen to your life here? Your job? Your holiday cottage, and us?'

'There is no guarantee I'll get the job, there may be a whole lot more applicants. I must submit it to Mr Tissa Fernando, the director of their wildlife department, and we will see if I'm successful. Would you come with me, and perhaps stay in some accommodation over there?' Digby tried to sound convincing, but Zelma could feel the trepidation in his voice.

'I need to tell you that I suffer from an airline flying phobia. Aviophobia, is what they call it.... however, will I get on a plane? I don't think I want to go into a country, with flies, dust, unbearable heat, and a language barrier. I'm a city girl – that would be totally alien to my nature! And what about the danger of the enterprise? They are criminals you are trying to apprehend. I can't believe I'm hearing you. A developing country has poverty, and with poverty there is crime.'

'Well, the contract is just for a few weeks; I don't even know what my chances are.' Digby walked up and down the deck, but he knew he had to win her over, if indeed he did get the job. 'Besides,

I'm sure there is treatment for your aviophobia. This is news to me. Let's go down the road for a walk. It will help to clear our heads.'

After breakfast they went for a leisurely country road walk, holding hands and each with their own thoughts. Zelma angry at the stupidity of his plan, and Digby determined to try and convince her that this is what he really wanted to do.

Coming back, they sat down to work things out. Digby told her how he would organise things in Australia with his parents and Scott helping. His employer might not be as easy to convince seeing that he had only worked there for a few months. This was a once in a lifetime opportunity, is how he saw it. But Zelma was furious at his planned stupidity. They spent the weekend clearing out the old shed of all unwanted and broken items, taking them down to the tip, trying to work out this newfound proposition of Digby's.

'There is no regular rubbish collection out of town, unless we engage a private rubbish collection; so, it is off to the tip with our garbage, where we have to separate the items, putting them into clearly marked areas,' Digby informed Zelma. This was a new experience to her. Country living was not for the faint hearted, Zelma was beginning to realise.

The rest of the day was spent collecting wood from the distributor in town, and just relaxing, before heading back home.

●●●

Returning to Melbourne, he carefully planned his application, making sure he mentioned his early life in the country, and his frequent trips to the wildlife parks with his parents and grandparents. His safari hunting trip with his uncle, and his ability to speak the Sinhala language, albeit not very fluently. He also talked about his deep hatred of poachers, and a lifelong desire to help apprehend them.

Two weeks later, Digby received the good news that he was called up for an interview with Tissa Fernando, and two other Wildlife Department officials, to be held in a week's time.

He understood there was another applicant with good references, and credentials, who was also being considered. He was a local to Sri Lanka, with a wide knowledge of wildlife, and its parks, but he was older, and possibly had some health issues. Digby was left sweating on his chances. He phoned his uncle Fred who was living in Sri Lanka and asked his advice on possible scenarios that could be thrown at him.

'Digby, my boy, always keep a calm disposition during the interview, don't take anything for granted, and don't be arrogant or cocky. You have youth, and experience working with me. Mention that if you like at the interview.'

He researched the modus operandi of poachers in other parts of the world, especially in Africa and India. They used cruel traps with wire netting, and bows and arrows poisoned with berries. This was the preliminary information he gathered, but there was more research to be done, if he was selected.

The day of the interview arrived done remotely via electronic media. Digby tried to be as prepared as he could, without sounding too nervous.

'Good morning, Digby, could you tell us why you think you are qualified to do this job?' Tissa greeted him.

'Well, I joined my uncle in his hunt for the notorious man-eating leopard of Vakarani, which we successfully killed. I lived in Sri Lanka until I was twelve years old and joined my grandparents often on trips to Yala and Wilpattu. I've been shooting for many years, and have joined the Sporting Shooters' Association of

Australia, keeping up my shooting skills. I hate poachers with a vengeance as they stole my pet baby elephant gifted to me by a family friend, when I was seven years old. I also have a basic knowledge of the Sinhala language.'

The three board members seemed pleased with that answer but went on. 'Killing a wild animal is different than capturing poachers. We hope you realise that.'

Another asked him, 'Tell us what you know about poaching methods.'

'Well, there are different cruel methods poachers employ. The wire noose is one. It's dangerous and terrifies the elephant, as the trunk is often caught and gets severely damaged, and it will die of starvation, as the trunk is necessary for everything it eats. Bows and arrows are another. The arrows are poisoned with berries taken from where branches are cut and boiled down into a treacle and attached to the arrows, where only a wound on an animal from these arrows will kill. In alleged defence of non-existent crops killing of animals takes place.'

'What do you know of the wildlife parks in the Island?'

'There are three large parks and several smaller ones; the largest being Yala, Wilpattu and Gal Oya, and I have visited all of them with my parents.'

'Good. Do you have any questions of us?'

'Yes, I have one. Is there any insurance cover against injury, or even perhaps, the remote possibility of death?'

'Well, as the American Wildlife Protection Society is involved, they will attend to that aspect of the contract. So, I'm sure that will be covered. We will inform you in two weeks as to the outcome of your application.'

He had been quizzed on all aspects of wildlife habits and habitats, as well as on the parks where the proposed contract was to take place. They threw practical hurdles at him, and he felt he was able to come up with some good solutions – albeit in his mind.

After an agonising two week wait, he was delighted to hear that he had been selected, with work to commence in a month's time. Tissa wanted Digby to connect with a Wildlife Officer and learn of wild animal behaviour, to be done either in Melbourne, or Sri Lanka. The work was to start in the dry season, which would be autumn in Australia.

•••

A workshop on Asian animals in the wild and on poaching methods used, was being held in Melbourne three weeks before his departure, which he planned to attend. In the meantime, there was plenty of preparatory work to be done.

His boss had to agree to his period of absence; his parents and Scott between them to overlook his weekender, which may require a short-term tenant, Scott to cover his crop-dusting piloting work, and most importantly, Zelma to be convinced that this is what he wanted to do.

Digby met up with Zelma the night he received the good news. He was on cloud nine, but unsure of her reaction. He planned a candlelight dinner at his apartment.

Zelma arrived, looking as glamorous as always. She sensed an important announcement from Digby. He was in no hurry to break the news, so they sat down to a roast meal he had prepared. After dinner sitting on the couch, he gently held her hand, and spoke softly.

'Zelma, my love, I heard today from Tissa Fernando that I have been selected for the position of conservationist, and team leader to apprehend poachers. The job starts in a month's time. I would really like you to come with me, even for a short while, if you can possibly manage it.'

Zelma went pale and was breathing rapidly, feeling nauseous. She started sweating, and hoped she wouldn't have a panic attack, as then she wouldn't be able to take in anything that Digby was saying. She poured herself a vodka, and took sips of it, trying to comprehend what he had just said. She felt she couldn't talk, or she may vomit. She was nervous and tense, and Digby was trying to understand her. She had to leave him for a while and go into the bathroom, retching, with a rapid heartbeat. This felt all wrong to her.

'Do you want to think about this and maybe we can talk at length another time?' he gently asked, to which she could only nod in agreement. They cuddled on the couch; he took her in his arms and kissed her again and again. She felt hot between her legs, and he slowly lay her down on the bed. 'I love you so much, and I will miss you even more when we are apart. Let's just live in the moment.'

She felt calm. He had that way about him that could calm her down, and after a while her panic eased, leaving her feeling happier, but she would need to get away to quietly comprehend what he had just said.

Zelma left a short while later, to try and digest all that was going on.

•••

Zelma woke the next morning after a restless night — she had a job to get to and needed to distract herself from the conversation of the night before. However, she needed to have a discussion with Digby, which would take all her resources to navigate. Going on the trip with him would not really work out, so she reasoned. He had a job to do, and she imagined she would only be in his way. That evening Zelma had a quiet dinner at her apartment.

Digby arrived on time, casually dressed as he always was, in jeans and open necked shirt, with smart trainers. Over dinner Zelma brought up what was on both their minds.

'I've given your trip some thought in between work, today. I don't think I can make it over until I get treatment for my aviophobia. I'll enrol with a psychologist as soon as I can. I believe it takes quite a few sessions. Are you sure you know what you are going into? It's a dangerous undertaking, in my eyes. The poachers are criminals and will stop at nothing to get their way.' She was wringing her hands and breathing deeply. 'There are diseases you need to protect yourself against. Going into the jungle and staying in primitive accommodation isn't like staying in a five-star hotel. Malaria, encephalitis, gastro-enteritis. hepatitis, and who knows what else, are all floating around in developing countries,' Zelma almost exploded. 'This is really a hair-brained scheme of yours, and I worry for you. We are thousands of miles away.'

Digby tried to placate her by putting an arm around her, but she wasn't in the mood for his peace offering and moved away ever so slightly. They both poured themselves a drink, he a scotch, she a vodka, and sat in silence.

'I realise your angst, darling; I will take all precautions I assure you and will look forward to you joining me, perhaps at the end of the assignment.'

It was an awkward silence for both. He was sure he was doing something he always wanted to, she felt she would feel isolated and so alone once he was away. Communication would be sporadic, is what she figured, especially when in a jungle he would have no mobile signal, which would make her worry even more. She needed to get therapy for her fears, as soon as she could, and get on a plane to be with him.

•••

Life went on at the Trott family farm. It was time to prepare the soil for planting snow peas. John got into his tractor and drove it rather fast making it hit a mound and roll sideways trapping John underneath part of the carriage. Gladys heard the commotion and rushed out on hearing John's screams.

'My God, I'll call the fire brigade and an ambulance,' she screamed out to him.

Returning to him he screamed, 'I can't feel my legs. I can't move them.'

In no time the ambulance and fire brigade were on the scene and rushed him to the local hospital. After sedating him an air ambulance was organised to take him to a Melbourne hospital. Gladys travelled with him and informed Digby.

'I have some very bad news. Your father is now in hospital in Melbourne after a farm accident where his tractor rolled over pinning him under, and it seems like his legs are affected. Come over as soon as you can.'

'Oh, my goodness, that's terrible news. I'm coming over immediately.'

After the surgery when John had somewhat recovered from the anaesthesia, he tried to comprehend what had happened. 'I remember the tractor rolling and being pinned under it, but very little else, other than loss of the feeling in my legs.'

Digby looked at his father with tears welling in his eyes. 'I'm trying to comprehend all this. I sincerely hope the loss of your legs is temporary and can be fixed.'

The usually morose and grumpy John was now even more grumpy. 'I'm shattered. Why me? Don't I deserve some happiness?'

Gladys looked on soulfully. 'Let's talk to the doctors, maybe this is temporary.'

Doctor Smith saw John and told him many more tests needed to be done. 'There is a chance, with rehabilitation, he could walk again. Only time will tell.'

John sat up in his wheelchair. 'I sincerely hope so. I've got a farm to run.'

Digby came in to see John while Gladys was there with him.

'Come here to gloat! No, I shouldn't have said that. I'm not in the best of moods today.'

'No Dad, I came here to see how you are going, but I'll leave if you rather I did.'

John looked downcast and away from him, offering no comment. Gladys held John's hand trying to control her tears; she had no words.

John went on, 'Son, you must go on your overseas trip after all the effort you have put into it.'

'Dad, I must try and adjust to all that has happened so suddenly. It will be better if we all had a good night's sleep and meet again at this hospital in a day's time with some thoughts on all that has happened.'

Digby went home to talk to Zelma and Scott. Zelma came over to his apartment. This needed a close conversation. 'I'm not sure what to do. Dad says I must go ahead with my trip; my mind may not be in the right place. I have a few weeks left before I leave. I could ask for a week or two postponement, but I'm now committed.'

'It may be best to get the doctor's opinion on how bad the injury is. If John can manage the farm with hired help and Gladys thinks she can manage, then go ahead and continue with your plans,' Scott said.

'Dad seems much more irritable; I guess he has a lot going on to deal with.'

Digby visited John when Gladys wasn't around for a close chat, but John had drifted off to sleep. He met his treating doctor who couldn't give him a clear indication of how John would respond, and when they would know of his long-term prognosis. That left Digby none the wiser, but still determined to make the trip as he had planned, perhaps, slightly delayed by a couple of weeks.

SIX

PREPARATION FOR THE TRIP

Scott was pursuing his vigilante work on Jack, who was not seen too often at his home in Morwell, so Scott decided to travel to Traralgon to pursue his instincts. His first port of call was the football club, where the barman knew Jack Smith.

The barman went on, 'He would get together with a few other young men, who would often be drunk and disorderly, and get into arguments. There was once a melee here and I had to call in the police. I haven't seen Jack for a couple of weeks. Being itinerant, he moves around. He has an aunt named Betty Smith who lives locally, and he occasionally stays with her. The locals may know where she lives,' and he summoned two young men to trace Betty's address.

Scott thanked the barman, and having secured the necessary address, he proceeded to meet Betty.

Betty was a small, neatly dressed lady, of about sixty-five years of age. She had twinkling eyes, and a weather-beaten skin, dressed neatly in appropriate clothes, of long pants and jumper, with work boots on. Her hair was of shades of grey, from milky white to dark grey, and cut short. She looked like she had been doing some gardening, and was wearing gardening gloves, when Scott arrived there unannounced.

'Good morning. May I introduce myself?' Scott said at the door. 'My name is Scott Taylor,' showing her his driving licence. 'I met Jack, your nephew, at the Traralgon Airport, where I work, and as he was looking for casual work, I may be able to help him.' Betty checked his driver's licence, and he filled her in on a few more details of how Digby and he met Jack. Betty invited Scott inside, as she felt he was trustworthy.

'Jack was here two days ago, but he moves around a fair bit, and never tells me where he is going. I just wait for him to turn up, and often to bail him out of trouble. Hope he hasn't been drinking or indulging in street drugs again. He is gullible, and gets in tow with criminals, and never seems to learn. He is like a son to me, after his mother died, and if you can help him, it will be a miracle.'

Scott was sympathetic to Betty's woes. Having met Jack only sporadically, he could feel her frustration. He wanted to bring Jack into Digby's life as he felt Jack could be a useful ally to him later, when Digby returned from the jungles. This made Scott determined to keep track of Jack's whereabouts.

'This is my card. Please call me when he turns up, I may be able to help him find work,' as he handed Betty his card and left.

•••

Digby was preparing for the workshop on Asian elephants, and other smaller wild animals. There was a wildlife adventurer running the workshop and Digby needed to have some background information, for which he was reading up on whatever books he could get hold of. The first part of the workshop was on the habits of elephants.

'Wild elephants are afraid of humans, and generally dislike man, they prefer their own deep jungle, and seldom damage crops or vegetables, unless they are food deprived. They are essentially harmless and timid by nature and are sensitive. In contradistinction, trained tame elephants have high confidence in man, and in supposed difference to the African elephant, the Asian elephant can be tamed. When close to an elephant it is essential to make as little noise as possible and have minimum of movement,' were the presenter's opening remarks.

There were people at the workshop who had personal experience with wild elephants, and one of them added some information. 'They always move upwind to locate any danger ahead. Cow elephants grow until the age of seventeen years, and their period of gestation is between eighteen and twenty-five months. I have been fortunate to witness elephants mating when in captivity. The male gets up on its hind legs, onto the back of the female in heat, and is almost vertical before penetration takes place.'

Digby wanted some information on *musth*.

The presenter went on '*Musth* occurs as a slight discharge of a strong-smelling fluid from the *musth* glands near the eye, directly above the line of the mouth. In younger males it occurs annually during the hot months, and during the mating season it lasts for two weeks, during which time the male is very temperamental, and can be ferocious, and attack on sight. The rare "rogue" elephant is savage, vicious and revengeful. 1 in 500 is a "rogue."'

Digby wanted to know, 'Does mating take place when the elephant in on *musth*?'

'Not always. From the age of about forty-five to fifty- five years *musth* disappears. Never trust an elephant on *musth*.'

Digby asked, 'Can you tell us something on the reproduction of elephants?'

'Certainly. Female elephants have on average four calves in their lifetime – twins are not uncommon, and the period of productivity is between ten and even up to fifty years of age. There is bellowing and trumpeting of wild elephants at night to protect the mother and calf from intruders, the noise being terrifying. Another female called the "aunt" will help to raise the young; the mother and the aunt will suckle the baby until five or six years of age. The aunt eats part of the afterbirth and will always accompany the mother and baby.'

One of the participants noted, 'I have seen large concentrations of perhaps hundreds of elephants during periods of drought, flood, or abundance of food.'

'Yes, a number of family groups and single elephants may join together into large concentrations of perhaps hundred elephants, the bonds within the family group being very strong.'

The workshop came to an end, Digby proposed a vote of thanks, and hung back to ask more questions.

'May I ask you a couple of questions, please? Herds, what can you tell me about them?'

'Herds usually consist of females, and it is after the monsoons that the full-grown male tuskers join the herd, but seldom enters the herd, and prefers to remain on the outskirts, within half-to-one mile of the herd. They have a yearly cycle of grazing grounds and follow the same tracks.'

'Also, please tell me about elephants charging.'

'When charging, an elephant trumpets and screams, throws sand over its body, and moves very fast up to twenty-five miles an hour. Its ears are spread out, head kept low, and trunk curled inwards, until the last second when it suddenly extends it.

Elephants can charge and stop suddenly, called *bluffing*. If in the path of a charging elephant, and running away, it has the scent of man, and rumour has it that if an article of clothing is left in its path, it may well attack the garment. To stop a charging elephant, one must shout and yell, easier said than done! A sign that an elephant is about to charge is that its tail starts twisting. Get away as fast as possible!'

Digby was satisfied that he had a fair amount of information on elephants; he also needed to get some information on *leopards*, and the jungle cat. The local library seemed to be his best resource.

SEVEN

THE ADVENTURE BEGINS

There was plenty to do organising his affairs in Victoria; a leave application to his boss for six weeks, some with pay and some on no pay; have an agent care for his weekender and a neighbouring farmer care for three sheep he owned. John suggested that he rent out the house to bring in some income and pay his mortgage. Scott had readily agreed to cover for him with weekend flying and crop dusting, so he called him.

'Scotty, I am over the moon, now that I got the position in Sri Lanka and start in about three weeks' time. There is plenty to tee up here, and things will be organised by Tissa Fernando at the other end. Zelma is far from happy at my going, and I hope she will come round to it as time passes. Thanks a million for covering for me, I owe you one!'

'No worries, mate, keep me in the loop. I can go over to your cottage in Mirboo now and again, especially keeping in touch with the agent, and your parents. I wish you all the best. Take care of yourself.'

His boss was sympathetic towards Digby's noble intentions but had some reservations as to the possible dangers involved, which he didn't vocalise. He did, however, say that as Digby was a recent employee there couldn't be any extensions and made sure he was aware of the conditions of the leave.

Digby was ecstatic at the great adventure that lay ahead, realising that this was a once in a lifetime assignment. The language barrier would not be too onerous, as most Sri Lankans, except for the villagers, spoke English, so he was made to understand. The food he had grown up on; rice and milder curry, was a favourite. He needed to carry a rifle and revolver and get a permit for them in Colombo.

He checked his resources on the *leopard and jungle cat* at the local library, and learnt that the leopard very rarely attacks man, is mostly a killer of domestic animals, such as sheep, goats and dogs; they only kill in the dark (as opposed to tigers which kill in daylight.) In the jungle, unlike a cheetah, it does not chase its prey, but relies on agility for a sudden pounce, charging unexpectedly, out of nowhere. It is full of mystery, makes little or no noise, and when it does pounce on its victim, the throat is torn out, and blood drunk as it flows from the wound. To follow a leopard, it's spoor or scent is required.

The jungle cat is also a target for poachers. They have a sandy grey coat, long legs, big ears, and a short tail barred with black. They are mini leopards and move like leopards. They are supreme hunters, and do not purr like domestic cats, hunt at dawn and dusk; small mammals, birds and lizards, being their prey.

Digby reckoned he had sufficient information for his trip. Now, for collecting a suitable wardrobe of tropical clothes, some with long sleeves, to protect against mosquitoes, and some in jungle camouflage, and most importantly, insect repellent spray. His course of inoculations against tropical diseases had to be completed, and the necessary documentation complied with. Authority to travel with guns also a necessity, at both ends of his travel.

•••

The days were drawing close to his departure, Digby and Zelma both getting excited; Zelma having mixed emotions at the thought of being left behind, and Digby daydreaming of what could lie ahead. Easter weekend was spent at Digby's cottage. It was a nostalgic weekend for the loved-up couple. On Thursday night he collected Zelma, and they headed off on the highway, for the two-hour trip to his cottage in Mirboo North. It was a rainy day, sheets of rain hitting the windscreen, whilst listening to the sentimental music on his radio. While Zelma looking out of the window, Digby remarked, 'A penny for your thoughts?'

'This is a nostalgic drive; I so wish you were not leaving.'

Digby turned to glance at her, a tiny tear falling down her cheek. He reached out and squeezed her hand, not quite knowing what to say to make her feel better. Being just ten minutes from their destination he kept on driving: a difficult time for both.

•••

Arriving at the cottage, he noted that his sheep were well cared for by the neighbour. They loaded up some wood from the shed and fired up the wood heater.

'Zelma, love, I believe we've got a bit of a mouse problem in the shed, there are mice droppings everywhere. After we've transported the sheep to Morwell, we'll have to put some mouse bait down, that should knock them out.'

Being a lovely moonlit night, the fragrance of freshly mowed grass filled the air; they sat on the deck looking at the traffic meandering down the highway in the distance, counting the stars in the night sky. She was on his lap, and stroking his head, a poignant time for both. Her eyes filled with tears dropping on his shirt. 'I will have to make it my mission to join you as soon as I can. I can't wait.'

Soon they lay down for a night of romance, she cradled his head, and he with his arms around her.

The next morning, they loaded the sheep into his trailer, and headed to Morwell a twenty-minute drive away, and for lunch at his parents' farm for a barbeque.

Arriving at the farm, John tried to lighten the conversation. 'Digby, are you now all set for your big adventure? Any last-minute nerves, second thoughts?'

'Definitely not, Dad. I will be in touch with Fred, and ask his advice, if needs be. I know he has gone through some adventures himself. You remember how the wicked poachers stole my baby elephant, gifted to us by those wealthy neighbours of Grandad? I hate them with a vengeance and can't wait to take my revenge on them. Scott has organised a tenant for the cottage, which is useful. Maybe Mum and you need to keep a quiet eye out there, just in case, and keep in touch with the agent. The neighbours too are friendly, and as you know country folk look out for each other.'

John nodded in agreement; he already had his work cut out looking after his farm and wasn't sure he'd have time for more work, in his present predicament, but didn't intend to upset his son.

Lunch was informal and quiet. Zelma appeared to get on well with Gladys and John, and they seemed to like her.

'Zelma dear, please keep in touch with us when Digby is away, as I understand telephone reception is not the best in the jungles of Asia, and we are in a valley here, so not too easy to reach either.'

'Definitely, will do so, Gladys, I'll need as much of your support from you as I can get.'

Lunch being over, the young couple decided to keep going, there was much to do at Digby's cottage.

On Easter Sunday, they cleaned up the cottage in readiness for the tenant, walked along the dirt road outside their house holding hands, met up with the farmer next door, who readily agreed to keep an eye on the cottage, and generally relaxed before Digby's trip on Monday.

•••

On Monday they left early for Digby's flight out of the Melbourne Airport, for the ten-hour direct flight into Colombo. Zelma looked at planes landing, remembering that she was supposed to get the feel of an airport as often as possible, to help her work through her fear.

After checking in his baggage, they wandered around the airport, Zelma imagining how she might overcome her fears, it seemed a monumental task to her. It was a tear-jerking farewell for them both, especially Zelma who was being left behind – she felt alone and lonely without him, driving back to her apartment. She phoned Joan as she arrived, feeling that she needed her mother's support more than ever, and planned a visit as a matter of priority. The motivation for seeing a psychologist to treat her fears stronger than ever and to re-unite with him as soon as she could.

•••

His plane touched down into Colombo International Airport at midnight., the hot humid air of the tropics striking his face as he walked out of the plane. His baggage had to be checked for bombs, weapons, and other dangerous instruments, but two guns were permitted for his specific purpose. Having changed his dollars into rupees, and cleared by customs, he emerged into the arrivals area to be met by Dhanasiri his driver, amidst crowds of people in the waiting area, all chattering away. Digby was tired and not in a loquacious mood.

'Hope you had a good flight, sir.'

'Yes, thank you, Dhanasiri, I am tired, and do want to hit my pillow. How far is the hotel?'

'About an hour's drive, sir.'

'Oh, good. I will nap till then.'

The night drive on quiet Colombo roads with hardly any traffic, was pleasant. Not too many dogs or cattle to slow down progress. They arrived at his destination in no time while he dozed. Booking in was swift and efficient, and his passport checked.

Digby's room at the luxurious hotel by the sea was large, with an attached lounge, overlooking the sea, the very relaxing sound of the pounding surf soothing to his ears. After a quick shower he hit the hay and was asleep in no time. He woke to the sound of birds and crows cawing, so typical of Colombo. He saw the rising sun – a giant ball of copper reflecting red and yellow on the horizon over the sea colour. The mist was a yellow haze, amidst the white clouds on a blue sky. The water was calm with the waves gently braking on the shore, the coconut palms swaying majestically in the breeze, taking in all the tropical beauty, whilst he had an early morning cup of tea. Native boys were already running along the shore chasing a rubber ball. Throngs of people were out enjoying a walk in the coolness of the early morning, on the splendid stretch of grass outside his hotel window. The heat of a tropical sun was still hours away. Street food a-plenty was being peddled by enterprising men pushing carts along the road with all types of mouth-watering delights inside them. The ever-present taxi drivers, and three-wheeler or *tuk tuk* drivers, were already lining up outside the hotel waiting for a fare. There was a buzz of tropical life which Digby found nostalgic and brought back memories of his childhood. The day was going to be mesmerising, sunny, and calling out for adventure.

Colombo being behind Melbourne in time, Digby called Zelma. 'Hello, my love. I arrived safe and sound, after a rather bumpy flight. Am in a luxurious hotel, on the edge of the ocean, and am missing you heaps. Please start your therapy as soon as you can. I will be here for today, and then leave for the game parks tomorrow. It is hot and humid here, so will stay in the hotel. Will call again soon, love you.'

'Dad and Mum, just a short call to let you know I arrived safe and sound. I leave for the jungles tomorrow, all going well here. Please keep Scott informed.'

Before breakfast he decided to take a quiet walk around the hotel. Several boys and taxi drivers followed him, either seeking to sell a souvenir, or offer him a ride into the city. 'Want to go in my *tuk tuk* sir? Very cheap. I can take you to the city. Ten minutes to the city, sir.' Digby had to fend them off politely, trying out his Sinhala. 'Nahay, nahay.' (No, no)

A swim in the saltwater pool was invigorating, the sea far too dangerous with under water currents, and enormous waves. The day was to be spent lazing by the pool or resting in his room.

•••

Zelma had commenced her therapy with Lucy, first with counselling, and followed by gradual exposure to a simulated interior of a plane. She took some deep breaths and tried to focus on what Lucy was saying. 'Close your eyes, breathe deeply, and visualise the inside of a plane. You are about to take off, are strapped into your seat, and hear the captain's voice come over the sound system.'

'I feel nauseous, Lucy, I need to have a bucket at hand.' Zelma implored. 'Don't think I can focus on the plane interior. All I see is lights flashing in my head. I don't think I can do this. I'm a hopeless failure. How will I ever travel?' she swallowed hard, and her mouth went dry.

'This will take time, Zelma. It's a slow process. Always keep a brown paper bag at hand to breathe into, when you start to panic. Hold it over your nose and mouth and breathe into it. We call this exposure therapy, you need to go into the situation that makes you anxious, do it in small steps, and listen to soothing music on your headphones when you attempt the difficult situations. You can do it. There will be two sessions a week for a few weeks. I know you are in a hurry to overcome the fear, you must try hard, and not have a defeatist mindset. I will see you again in four days' time. Visit the airport on the weekend and observe the planes from the observation deck.'

Zelma dutifully kept doing all that Lucy recommended, and had a few weeks of therapy before her, as she didn't intend leaving for Colombo until Digby was coming to the end of his assignment, believing she would be a distraction to him.

•••

Breakfast downstairs, a banquet awaited Digby, of western and eastern food; stringhoppers and hoppers, served with a variety of curries, milk-rice, sambals, tropical fruit and drinks, not to mention all types of western food for the not so adventurous. A cup of freshly brewed tea after delicious tropical fruit of papaya, custard apple and sweet pineapple. After a hearty breakfast, he tried to catch up on his sleep from jet lag, as Tissa had given him a day for rest, which he soaked up appreciatively. He decided to take a walk outside the hotel on the enormous green lawn, often held for political rallies. The street hawkers were selling their prepared street food in carts, including enormous fried prawns on a lentil bun, or chickpeas fried in hot oil, tossed with chilli powder, and red chillies. Young lovers walking hand in hand, under an open parasol to hide their identity. The never-ending sound of horns, and absence of road rules on the main road abutting the green; the little fishing boats on the sea, and the ships sailing past on the horizon. He remembered all these scenes from his past and loved remembering. The morning heat was slowly turning into a humid day, and he was keen to get back to the cool of his room.

Tissa Fernando phoned Digby, mid-morning, 'Ayubowan (Hello) Digby, welcome to Sri Lanka, hope you are being well looked after. The plan is for Dhanasiri to drive you tomorrow morning, after breakfast to the circuit bungalow adjoining the Yala National Park, which is your first place of work. I will meet you tomorrow on your arrival into Buttala.'

'Ayubowan, Tissa. This accommodation is superb, thank you. I look forward to meeting you tomorrow.'

Digby spent the rest of the day sitting by the pool, talking to waiters trying to brush up on his Sinhala, or watching television, Colombo style. After a good night's rest, he left following an early breakfast, with Dhanasiri, to drive down south through Ratnapura the city of gems, stopping for a quick cuppa. Then on through Balangoda, passing paddy fields ploughed by buffaloes rather than modern machinery. Numerous maidens wearing cloth and jacket, were selling fresh cadjunuts recently harvested, and known as the 'cadju girls.' A lone elephant with a mahout walking along the road, together with stray dogs and cattle wandering along the road, had to be navigated, a loud horn a necessity. All along the road, wayside vendors sold basket ware, king coconuts, and fruit.

Lunch was at the small town of Belihul Oya, in the Rest House which always delighted Digby, since his childhood days. A wedding was in progress: the bride dressed in a colourful red sari, the groom in a sherwani type white shirt intrigued him. They sat at the bridal table having a meal of rice and curry. The stream outside the rest house with its sparkling clear water was tempting for a cool swim. Maybe another time, he reckoned. Then onwards towards Buttala, with dusk settling over the road, and no streetlights, a pair of magnificent elephants were trying to cross the road, making Dhanasiri brake in a hurry. It shook Digby out of his slumber.

'Strewth, Dhanasiri, that is a magical sight. We will have to wait for them to disappear into the jungle. Is this a common sight?'

Suddenly, the larger of the two pachyderms turned and came towards their vehicle with its trunk curled in front of its head, and bellowing loudly, while the other went into the jungle.

'My god, it's charging us. Reverse, reverse.' With tyres screeching Dhanasiri reversed the vehicle, both holding their breaths. The elephant then stopped suddenly, it had been bluffing. It took the two men a few minutes to regain their breath, and look up, to see that the pair had disappeared into the jungle. Accelerating as fast as he could, the driver whizzed past the spot with horn blaring, and on full beam head lights. The two men heaved a sigh of relief.

'It's a good thing I don't have a weak heart,' Digby kept saying again and again.

•••

Finally arriving at the small hamlet of Buttala, Tissa was waiting to meet them. He was tall, lean, tanned, with a friendly smile, and thick black wavy hair, well dressed in jeans, and casual shirt, about forty-five years of age, and had been the Manager of the Wildlife Department for ten years.

'Hello Digby, welcome to the jungles of Sri Lanka. You have a three-bedroom house for your use, which will also accommodate the staff who will be part of your team. A cook cum houseboy, a jeep driver, and two other men will be part of the team. A four-wheel drive vehicle is for your use. Please contact me if you need anything. The main target of the poachers besides elephant and leopard, more recently are Indian pangolins. There will be a fresh driver, Palitha, to take you into the park and for driving around the park, together with two other members of the team who you will meet in the morning. I will be in touch. Good night.'

The culture shock that greeted Digby was overpowering, even though he had lived there many years previously. The midday humidity, the hot nights requiring a fan or better still, an air conditioner. Having his meals prepared, and a chauffeur to take him around was something he could easily get accustomed to. In the morning he rose to see the rising sun colour the sky golden and purple and rosy, whilst the milky white clouds sped across the powdery blue sky. There was a soft breeze blowing through the tall coconut trees. His house had semi jungle around, with a deep well which provided water pumped up to the house.

A cacophony of wild birds, and a lone peacock's shrill call, were pure nostalgia. A little black bird jumped from stone to stone, and the red wattled lapwing or 'did you do it' kept it company, the *chik chaks* on the wall produced a sound so loud from which it gained its name; it was hard to believe that such a small lizard could produce such a loud noise. Several ducks were flying everywhere as it was duck season, whilst the ever-present monkeys were jumping from tree to tree. All this brought back memories to Digby, and he was thoughtfully remembering his childhood. The calls of more tropical birds lulled him to sleep.

EIGHT

INTO YALA NATIONAL PARK

After breakfast, the driver Palitha, together with Sunil and Bandara, two well-built young men, arrived in a vehicle to take him to the entrance of Yala National Park, where they met the Divisional Game Ranger. A park ranger cum guide had to travel in the vehicle, to guide and protect them from any potential danger.

'Sir, there are three blocks which the park is divided into,' the Game Ranger said. 'Only blocks one and two are open to the public. Block one has numerous elephants and is teeming with leopard. Block two, has a river flowing through it; during the monsoon, this river overflows and the park can't be navigated, but presently, it being the dry season, it is open. Having plenty of thick trees and shrubs, it is popular with poachers. Block three is closed to visitors, although poachers may use it for ganja (cannabis) cultivation. Altogether it is around two hundred and forty square miles in extent, with plenty of space for poachers to hide in.'

'Thank you. Today, and maybe tomorrow, we plan to drive

around blocks one and two, to get our bearings, to locate the watch huts, and generally get a feel of what the park is like.'

With the tracker, seated in front, they left along the bumpy, sandy road. No sooner than travelling a few hundred yards they came across the carcass of a dead elephant with its face cut away, and the tusks removed, Digby wanted to alight from the vehicle, but the tracker refused.

'No sir, rules are that no one can get out of the vehicles, except at certain areas. We can park the vehicle, and you can have a look from inside the vehicle,' the tracker insisted.

Going up to the animal the general opinion was that poachers must had killed it. 'We need to know how they did it. Was it by poisoning, or shooting or a wicked trap?' Digby said to the others.

Moving on they passed a crocodile basking in the sun, spotted deer by the dozen, a sambhur, and a peacock. As there were several other tourist vehicles in block one, they drove onto block two.

Being early in the morning, they heard the trumpeting of a herd of elephants, followed by the frightened bark of a spotted deer, and the high-pitched call of a peacock. Passing large thorny trees stunted by the heat, huge cactus, fleshy, green, and ominous looking, and giant leafless trees, thick bushes between the trees, with undergrowth full of decaying leaves, they kept driving deeper into the jungle. As they approached the middle of the day, the sun was relentless, and the air humid, with no sound from the animals. Turning a corner, they came upon a family of ten elephants in their road. The tracker instructed an immediate stop, reverse, and wait. He had to see what the animals would do next. They appeared oblivious of the watching human eyes, and the vehicle. Or so it seemed. There was always a watchman to protect the herd, and Digby observed, 'That young male is away from the herd and is watching us.'

The tracker added, 'Sir, his tail is twisting, that is not a good sign. He may charge. We must reverse.'

As Palitha put the car into reverse, the elephant headed towards them. The road branched, and he took the left fork, the elephant, thankfully, going straight.

'My god. That was a close shave,' one of the others said in relief. 'Let's just stop somewhere and catch our breath. What a close shave!'

With hearts beating out of their chests, they took stock of their bearings. Maybe it was prudent to drive by the river, park their vehicle, get out, and stretch their legs. The river was slow and meandering, and the water crystal clear. After a while they got back into their vehicle and set off to locate the watch huts where they would spend the night, watching and waiting for the crims. They were well camouflaged wattle and daub huts, covered with large palms and branches blending in well with the surroundings.

Digby commented, 'I'm sure there are snakes, scorpions and spiders all living in the rafters of those huts. We must closely look through the huts, before we are sitting ducks.'

The huts were on the periphery of the park abutting the sea. Looking inside Digby remarked,

'We'll need to bring all our necessities, as there are only camp beds here with mosquito netting, a couple of oil lamps and mosquito coils, and little else. Three people could fit in there.'

'Yes sir, I agree,' Palitha added. 'Water for drinking and washing as well, unless we go down to the river for washing. Cooking is with kerosene, which we must bring in. Latrines are only the pit variety.'

After having a look around, they passed a water hole where a herd of deer, ever vigilant, were drinking, necks down, peering up all the time to sense a lurking leopard slinking through the undergrowth, rightly too, as the team noticed a leopard hiding behind a bush; silence was imperative. Driving on they left for the barrier gate, to drop off the tracker and head back to the Buttala bungalow.

•••

After dinner Digby contacted Zelma, 'I had the most wonderful Cook's tour of the Yala Safari Park. It was tinder dry, and the animals were plentiful at the waterholes. It's not going to be easy locating the poachers, as there is dense jungle, and they could be hiding anywhere. We were charged whilst in our vehicle by a young bull elephant, which was both dangerous and exciting. The watch huts are very primitive, but this is jungle accommodation, so that's to be expected! Tomorrow night is our first watch for the poachers. It will be exciting; I'm looking forward to it.'

'Please be careful, my love. Those men are criminals, and I'm sure they know the jungle very well. I've started my therapy with Lucy, and it's going well. I should be able to fly soon. I love you.'

The next call was to his parents, giving them much the same information. He then hit his pillow for a good night's rest.

•••

On the next day, after an early breakfast, they set out once more for the barrier gate at Palatupana, to collect the necessary tracker, who was a different man, and progressed to block two. The jungle here being thick and dense, trees with enormous leaves, the acacia with feathery foliage, bamboo plants, and coconut trees made up the landscape. A small waterfall whispered and sighed, as the water fell like a bridal veil. Having brought some provisions, they contemplated whether it would be wise to leave them in the watch huts which were always open. Deciding against this, they kept on driving, when they noticed the carcasses of two dead elephants, with their tusks cut out.

'Those have been dead for about a week; their swollen bodies don't tell us how they died,' the tracker remarked.

'We have to inform Tissa,' Digby added. 'I'm sure he doesn't know of the number of dead elephants in the park.'

The jungle looked sinister and unwelcoming in the hot midday sun; they parked their vehicle under a large banyan tree and waited. It wasn't long before they heard footsteps rustling the undergrowth, and soft voices.

'Aiyoo putha (son) there are leopard prints on the ground here. It looks like there must be a leopard around somewhere.'

Three men emerged dressed in khaki camouflage outfits, armed with bows and arrows, and guns, were creeping around. The team spotted them, with binoculars. Digby watched them but had no authority to apprehend them, and just as they appeared they seemed to disappear into the jungle. The team waited another hour, but there was no sign of any men, so they quietly moved their vehicle away and drove around block two, enjoying a cut lunch they had brought with them. After lunch they returned to the spot under the banyan tree and waited. The three men returned about three pm, when they heard footsteps again. Digby and Palitha jumped out and confronted the men. As Digby didn't speak Sinhala, Palitha glowered at them in a barking tone of voice.

'What are you three doing here with guns and bows and arrows?'

'Aiyoo Mahatmaya, (sir) we are looking for a leopard and two cubs,' said the taller and most senior looking of them.

'What good is the gun unless you want to kill the animals? Get out of here, and if we catch you again walking around with weapons, we will take you to the police station.'

They decided returning to their base camp was necessary, to let Tissa know what they had seen, and to organise a warrant of arrest for suspicious characters. Tired, but content that some progress was being made, they enjoyed a cold beer at the local rest house. The barman wanted to talk, but they were all too tired for conversation, whilst a black cormorant darted and dived into the nearby reservoir.

On day three of their first assignment, they didn't enter the park, but waited to meet Tissa and organise the arrest warrant, and plans to locate other poachers, as Digby reckoned there must be quite a few. He woke up as usual at the sound of the birds calling each other and drank in the sounds of nature. After a typical Lankan breakfast, Tissa arrived.

Digby told him, 'Tissa, I think there is a well organised ring of poachers we are dealing with, three of them were in Block Two yesterday, and there are probably several others in Block Three. We need a special warrant for their arrest.'

Tissa responded, 'You will need special permission to access Block Three. I will investigate the possibility of the team going in there. You will need bullet proof vests. I will organise the urgent issue of a warrant, and please take your shot gun and pistol in with you.'

The Grama Sevaka or Village Headman organised the arrest warrant for the next day's trip into the Game Park. *I remember going into the Yala park in my childhood so vividly. It was just magical and not stressful.* That was under vastly different circumstances, he mused.

●●●

Day four saw the team all wake early. This was going to be an important day. They left after lunch, with provisions for dinner and breakfast. Digby had the necessary forms. The team of Palitha, Sunil and Bandara together with Digby collected a tracker at the gate, and once more drove through Block one. In Block two the sunlight was filtering through the thick trees and bushes, the jungle smelt of evil and foreboding making for a huge opportunity for poachers to carry out their evil trade. In block one they turned left at the Yala bungalow, and drove alongside the Menik River tributary, which slowly meandered as a small trickle of water. Tissa advised Digby that the poachers may camp on the Bagura Plains, and to approach the plains with caution when driving to the watch huts. In proximity to the camping grounds was a thick clump of trees and bushes where they planned to park, and they waited. It was dusk and the tracker had noticed some footprints in the dry earth.

Before long they heard footsteps and mumbling. A gang of about four youths naked to the waist, in loin cloths, came softly out of the jungle talking in Sinhala.

'Aiyoo, aiyoo, athay koo sathung?' Translation: 'Where are the animals today?'

They were armed with poisonous arrows, and two of them had rifles slung over their shoulders. They moved stealthily and bent low as if searching for something. The tracker, Digby, and Palitha quietly opened their car doors and stood beside the vehicle, as silently as possible. A shot rang out, they heard footsteps, voices and a cacophony of birds together with a flutter of wings, and the jungle was suddenly alight with hundreds of birds in the air. All of Digby's team raced towards the sound from where the shot rang out, to see a dying sambhur writhing on the ground, and the men around it. They then pounced on the men.

'Hora, hora, sathung maruwa.' (Translation: 'Thief, thief. Animal killer') Palitha shouted.

There were fisticuffs thrown around, with moonlight illuminating the undergrowth. The only way to identify the poachers was that they were bare footed and bare bodied. Digby got hit on the shoulder, and Palitha on the head, but the poachers also received a battering especially from Sunil and Bandara. All of them were bruised and bleeding, and three of them were handcuffed, but one of them escaped. Palitha, Digby and the tracker left with them for the Police Station, whilst the other two stayed in the watch huts, Digby left his rifle with them in case they were attacked. After an hour's drive they arrived at the Ampara Police Station where the three men were put into lock up, Digby and the others returned to join the other two. Arriving back, they found them awake and alert, and after a meal they all fell asleep, at about midnight. About one hour later there were flickering lights of torches and three men stood in the doorway. Sunil woke up and shouted, 'Help, these men are attacking us.' The others all jumped up and all hell broke loose. Crash, thump, smash, the men all went for each other. In the dark with only moonlight shining through the trees there was a melee like no other with men falling over each other. Digby switched on his powerful torch to apprehend the criminals, but on seeing the light they escaped into the jungle. Hurt and bruised they collected their belongings. 'Let's head back out of this trap – it's too dangerous sleeping here,' he announced to his team.

•••

When Tissa arrived that morning, he decided that there was little else to do at Yala. The bruises and wounds from the melee were not considered serious.

Digby approached Tissa. 'I believe that travelling from Buttala to the Gal Oya National Park would be too far. It would be best if a circuit bungalow there could be organised.'

'I agree, Digby. I will have a three-bedroom house organised for your team. If you need more strong men to help, I will have another vehicle, and two more well-built men to join your team.'

A postcard had arrived from Zelma, *It's nice hearing from Australia,* thought Digby.

He phoned Zelma before leaving Buttala. 'Hello love. Just leaving for our next stop after a successful trip in Yala. Three men were apprehended – there was a bit of a melee over two nights, not much damage done to life or limb. Hope we are more successful at the next stop.'

'I am so proud of you. Hope to be with you soon as I am progressing well with my therapy and will book my flight when I feel confident enough to travel. I will phone Gladys and let her know.'

NINE

INTO GAL OYA NATIONAL PARK

Tissa told Digby, 'I'll organise a circuit bungalow for the team at Inginiyagala. It will be within easy reach of the Gal Oya Park. In this park foot safaris are allowed. It's a smaller park and is completely land locked. There being large herds of elephants, as many as two hundred and fifty sometimes; this meant that they were targeted by poachers. The large reservoir provides a perennial source of water, and elephants congregate around the tanks.'

'A compass and a flare will be necessary, should we get lost. Kindly organise it, Tissa.'

After a few hours' drive, passing through Ampara for groceries, they arrived for lunch. As this area was in the dry zone, heat and humidity could be overwhelming. The house being situated on the edge of the jungle, the aroma of lush vegetation wafted into the house. The orchestra like sound of plentiful bird life, was a delight to Digby's ears. Memories of his childhood came flooding back. They decided to rest that night and await the arrival of reinforcements to their team the next day.

The next morning Digby and the others sat in the veranda listening to the sounds of the jungle, which was melodious. Thick with green bushes and trees, the green ranging from pale aquamarine to the deep colour of jade, magnificent and undisturbed in places, evil looking in others. This beauty disguised the danger lurking in the coming days.

After breakfast when the other two men and the additional jeep arrived, Digby called out, 'Let's get the show on the road. We must leave now to get to the barrier gate, a good half hour drive. Welcome to Anura and Gamini who will travel in the other vehicle with driver Sunil.'

The team set out after breakfast, to collect the tracker at the barrier gate. No tourists are allowed in this park, leaving it an easier target for poachers than in Yala. They proceeded along the bumpy and dusty road, the menacing jungle all around them. There was a herd of about a hundred elephants in the distance, under the shade of large trees, quite unconcerned at the watchful eyes. They proceeded to the watch huts at the periphery of the park and noted that they were dilapidated, and in need of mosquito proofing, and some cooking apparatus, smelling dusty and mouldy.

Digby remarked, 'We need a lot more here than we did at Yala and need to be well prepared. These are extremely basic huts, although they are hidden from people outside.'

Looking inside with powerful torches Palitha noticed an enormous python curled up in one of the rafters with the stench of dead rats. Being a snake handler, he climbed up and attempted to remove the python, but it just squirmed its way further into the thatched roof.

'We'd better not use this hut,' Digby informed the others. 'There are four more huts to choose from.'

They proceeded on their surveillance of the park, noticing leopard footprints in the sand.

The tracker remarked, 'The Park has got plenty of leopard in it now, it's breeding season.'

A boat ride on the Samudra Reservoir was necessary to locate further habitats of elephant, and where they could take the boat right up to the banks and investigate any camping sites of poachers. The reservoir grown over with water hyacinth with their delicate mauve flowers rooted in water, float along as their boat passed through making a channel of clear water. As soon as the boat had passed, they drift back with the breeze and no trace that the boat had gone that way remains. They did notice burnt embers of old fires, and evidence of recent activity near the water. The poachers were active and around. Another dead elephant carcass, with its tusks removed, all bloated, and stinking, dead for quite a few days was hidden under several trees.

Digby, once more, loved the atmosphere of the jungle, the lush green vegetation, and the never-ending sounds of birds. He felt all hyped up at the upcoming evening's agenda. With the heat of midday coming on, they returned to their vehicles for the trip back to base.

'We need to proceed to Amparai today for provisions, and all basic necessities for the night, but after lunch I suggest we all have a little siesta and reserve our energy for the evening trip.'

The trip to Amparai in the late morning sun with no air conditioning in the car was not too pleasant. To prevent the car overheating Palitha drove slowly making for a longer journey. With their supply of necessities, they journeyed back looking forward to the cool bungalow,

Palitha remarked, 'Sir, I hope we are well stocked now; no more long midday trips if we can help it!'

•••

That evening they set out in two vehicles, with all provisions, mosquito prevention and the all-important arrest warrant, for the entrance to the Gal Oya National Park. Collecting the tracker, they drove to the watch huts and set themselves up for the night. The jungle at night began to take on an eerie atmosphere, hundreds of fireflies were about, and it belied the dangers which lay within. A magnificent peacock with its tail outspread walked proud treading the ground with delicacy, grace, and elegance. There was a smorgasbord of wildlife for treacherous poachers, and they had to be around somewhere in the park.

The setting sun was golden across the pale blue sky, with white powder puff clouds floating across it interspersed with dark clouds. A clap of thunder shattered the silence, Digby voicing his fears, 'I feel a hundred eyes are watching us. It is eerie and unpredictable, and any rain will not be helpful.'

Foot safaris were permitted, but every stick could be a snake, and they all wore heavy boots. They continued their journey in silence, for the jungle conveyed sounds like a loudspeaker, they had to be super quiet. Another half hour drive and out stepped a magnificent tusker ahead of them, secretions dripping from its upper face, near its eyes. It was in musth and highly dangerous, dragging his trunk on the ground. He stopped and faced them, curled his trunk, and looked menacing, ready to charge. The tracker leaned out of the vehicle, showed an open hand, and yelled out 'Goya, Goya.' This made the beast stop in its tracks look at them long and hard, and move slowly to the side, and walked into the jungle. Palitha began to reverse; they were all dumbfounded, unable to speak and trembling in fear.

They reached the two watch huts and set up for the night, and noticing a small cave to the north of the huts, 'Maybe an animal or two would be resident inside it,' Digby muttered to Palitha.

True to his word, a sloth bear with two cubs had made it their home; the shy animals not emerging until the commotion had died down in late evening. They made a handsome family, Digby's team keen not to invade their privacy.

Inside the huts, once set up, they took some liquid nourishment and food, sprayed on insect repellent, and waited. Their vehicles well camouflaged by the trees; they fell asleep in the huts one by one; the cool air a perfect hypnotic.

It must have been midnight when the sound of an elephant trumpeting nearby woke them in fear. They moved to the veranda, where they saw the lights of several torches about five hundred metres away. They decided to go out and investigate. The rains had stayed away, and a new moon was shining through the trees.

'Go in single file,' Digby whispered. Only the fireflies with their glowing lights buzzing around lit the way. A gunshot rang out and a cacophony of squawking birds flew out of trees, whilst the team raced towards the sound of the shot. There lay a magnificent elk with its horns in velvet writhing in agony, and then the poachers jumped on Digby's men. The poachers were dressed in dark clothes, five in total, and were bare footed, easier to distinguish from the others in boots. Digby was walloped and pounded, hit on the back of his head. He stumbled forward, reeling, and swinging blindly. He threw wild punches but didn't make contact, just hitting through air, his shoulders sore from swinging wildly. He felt like he would never breathe again, with lights flashing before his eyes. He tried his karate leg swings, but was stumbling, sweating, and with his heart racing, was not gaining much of an advantage. He could sense that the others were in a similar situation, but the seven excluding the driver who stayed away, outnumbered the five poachers.

He heard someone shout, 'Yakoo, koheda anith thenna?' (Translation – Devil, man, where are the others?)

In the dark there was mayhem, men falling on top of each other, swearing and shouting. Some of them ran off into the jungle, but three men were tackled to the ground. These three were handcuffed and led away by bruised and injured men from Digby's team, who were not in prime condition themselves. An uninjured Bandara and the tracker led the way using torches, back to the watch huts, to take stock. It looked like the walking wounded. Applying first aid dressings, three of them drove the captured poachers to the nearest police station, the uninjured tracker being a necessity to travel with them. After placing the three criminals in police lockups a police patrol car accompanied them back. In the meantime, it was assumed that the elk was dying or already dead, unless the two escaped poachers returned to claim their trophy. They all fell asleep exhausted, the rest of the night being eerily quiet.

●●●

With the onset of dawn, so tranquil in the heart of the jungle, they woke to the sound of the birds, and the occasional bark of a frightened deer. A loud shrill peacock's call was always to be heard, the best alarm clock anywhere. Digby and Palitha managed to hobble along to check on the injured elk, but it had disappeared, taken by a wild animal, or the remaining poachers. There were branches from broken tree trunks, plenty of footprints and deep troughs of earth from the melee of the night before. Some blood stains on the ground from the many injured men, and the dead elk. All Digby's men had headaches from the battering they had received, Digby himself aching all over his body, with welts and bruises just beginning to appear, they returned to the huts for a light breakfast and a cup of tea, after which they packed up to return to the Inginiyagala circuit bungalow.

•••

Battered and bruised, Digby's team rested, waiting for further instructions from Tissa. The Minneriya National Park was supposedly teeming with elephant, but it being over a hundred kilometres from Gal Oya, Tissa left it to Digby to decide whether they wanted to stay two nights there. They decided against it, preferring to be fresh for the trip into the Wilpattu Park, and as the poachers didn't seem to be present at Minneriya. Instead, they would rest where they were, and proceed to the most dangerous of all parks at Wilpattu.

'Tissa, I believe snakes and Indian pangolins are now targeted as well, both for their meat and as pets, it is imperative that we break this poaching racket.'

'Yes, Digby, the same team will move on in two days' time. The poachers who were captured are maintaining a stony silence. They will not divulge who the ring leaders are, and we don't want to use severe tactics to make them talk. Let's wait and see.'

'Tissa, there is another matter which bothers me a bit. I'm just wondering if there is someone in my team who is relaying information to the poaching master minds? It seems to be more than coincidental that they always know where we will be for the night. Everybody in my team appears loyal… but I just wonder. Thought I'd get your input on that.' Digby was pursuing all avenues, as to how the poachers knew their plans and movements.

Tissa was taken aback; he believed he had hand-picked his men and could rely on them for loyalty. 'Hmm. I hadn't thought of it, but now that you mention it, I'll investigate it.'

•••

Digby phoned Zelma, 'Hello beautiful, had a rather bruising night yesterday. Three of us got beaten up, seven of us against their five, but we managed to capture three of them who are now in custody. I believe we're making some ground in catching poachers, but the ring leaders are difficult to locate; the men refuse to talk. We leave in two days for the largest park, the Wilpattu Game Park, in the northwest section of the island, which will be challenging.'

'Oh Digby, my love, I'm truly worried about you. I have almost completed my course of treatment and will book my plane ticket and accommodation in Colombo. I will need somewhere to stay in proximity to the Wilpattu park, so any suggestions from Tissa would be welcome. I will decide to fly out in the coming days and will call you with definite plans.' She had a sixth sense, or maybe feminine intuition that he was in danger.

'Yes, love, I do look forward to seeing you again. It is very hot and humid here, please bring light clothes and sandals. Lots of sunscreen lotion and a wide brimmed hat. I will eagerly wait to hear from you again.'

TEN

ZELMA TAKES A PLANE TRIP

Zelma was concerned at the sporadic contact with Digby, as he did not give away much as to what exactly was happening in the jungle. No doubt he was in danger. Gladys, John, and Scott knew little of what was happening, and Zelma had to convey the scanty information she had to them. His rural property was being well cared for, as were his shifts at the airport. She certainly knew she had to meet him before his next trip into the Wilpattu jungle. She applied for three weeks leave and booked her flight for the weekend coming up.

Now for the plane journey. This was what she had been preparing for these past few weeks. She would need to organise a car and driver in Colombo, together with all her accommodation. Her airline ticket had to be purchased; she preferred a small passenger cabin in the plane.

She called Digby, 'Hi there, my darling, I am leaving on Saturday this weekend; could Tissa please organise the Colombo hotel you used, plus pick up from the airport, and transport for all my travels, as well as my stay in proximity to the Wilpattu park. I am so looking forward to seeing you, but first I must make the dreaded plane flight, an eleven-hour nonstop journey, arriving at midnight. Flight details are in my email to you. See you soon my love, can't wait.'

Her flight left Melbourne in the afternoon; she reserved an aisle seat, on the upper deck of the plane. She had her list of instructions from Lucy, her brown paper bag to breathe into if she started panicking, and a small rubber ball to keep squeezing to relieve her tension. She went through a last-minute session with Lucy to help deal with the panic beginning to rise as her departure drew nearer.

On this important Saturday, in the afternoon she took a taxi to the airport and fronted up at the information counter to ask for guidance. There were throngs of people everywhere, and Zelma was beginning to feel overwhelmed. Lucy had told her to close her eyes and calm herself down when her heart started racing. She was breathing rapidly, her palms sweaty, and her heart starting to race. Standing in the queue seemed a long-drawn-out process, but hoorah, she was at the check-in counter, handed over her ticket and passport, and waited for confirmation of her seat. So far so good! Her hand luggage was checked for weight and size, and she was then given her baggage receipt and boarding pass, plus the number of the boarding gate and time of boarding. Two hours to go before boarding, next stop was a café for coffee, and a quiet seat somewhere to try and relax, and put her relaxation tape on. This was the ultimate test she had been preparing for. To go into a panic attack now would be too humiliating. She kept repeating to herself, *keep calm, keep calm, you can do this, you can do this.*

*E*ventually she was heading through the double doors of the departure terminal, past the duty-free shops, and towards the boarding gates. She could not sit still and had to keep moving.

Then found a quiet spot, sat down, and turned on her relaxation tape. A text to Digby might be a clever idea and a diversion. Then he called her.

'Love, how are you faring? We are about to pack up here and make the trip to Puttalam.'

'Oh Digby, it's so good to hear from you. I have checked in and am seated here trying to psyche myself up to going into the plane and make the trip. I do hope it all goes well, and I don't collapse in the plane!' Zelma was feeling the pressure.

'I'm sure you'll be fine; you've done all the demanding work, and it will pay off. I'll talk to you in Colombo and see you when you arrive in Puttalam. I'm so proud of you being able to make this trip. Love you heaps.'

The boarding lounge being open, Zelma went through to be checked for liquids and metal objects. There was half an hour to go before entering the plane, so she sat quietly and imagined a tranquil scene, closed her eyes, and tried to meditate, but it was too noisy around her. Not being able to sit, she stood and stretched her long limbs.

Soon it was time to board, to stand in a queue, have her boarding pass and passport checked; then dragging her hand luggage she was directed to her seat. Placing her hand luggage in the overhead compartment, with a deep sigh, she sat in the aisle seat, and strapped herself in. The seat next to her was taken by a quiet young man, who made no attempt of chattering throughout the flight; thank goodness for that, is what she reckoned.

•••

Some minutes later the lights were dimmed, and the pilot's voice came over the speakers.

'Good afternoon, ladies and gentlemen, I am your Captain, Harsha de Silva speaking. Welcome aboard, we have clear weather ahead, and should have a good trip over the next few hours. Fasten your seat belts for a smooth take off and contact the cabin crew should you need anything.'

Zelma was starting to feel queasy in the stomach, and felt dizzy; her palms were beginning to become sweaty, and she felt herself mildly hyperventilating. She set up her relaxation tape and had her brown paper bag ready to breathe into if she continued hyperventilating. Beginning to feel nauseous she swallowed an anti-nausea tablet. *Breathe deeply, breathe deeply,* she kept repeating to herself. Slowly the plane was taxing forward on the runway, the engines put into full throttle, and quietly the plane started ascending. She closed her eyes and held tightly onto the arm rests of the seat. Her heart beating fast, she worried about getting a heart attack on the plane. Deciding she was too young for that, she concentrated on the exercises Lucy had taught her, and switched on her tape.

In no time the plane was above the clouds and cruising, ascent had been negotiated, she told herself. I have done that part of the trip. *Calm down,* she kept telling herself. The relaxation tape was so peaceful, she decided she could now relax.

Turbulence on the flight needed her to go through this all over again; eating or drinking was initially refused in case she didn't retain it. She tried to sleep, even though it was five o'clock in the evening. All she could do was listen to calming music. She tried reading a novel, but the words were skimming in front of her eyes; she tried a crossword puzzle, again with little success.

An hour later the main meal was being served. 'Fish or chicken?' the flight attendant asked her. She chose fish not even sure if she could eat anything for fear of nausea; and just picked at her meal. After the meals were cleared, the lights were dimmed, but Zelma couldn't fall asleep. Instead, she closed her eyes and tried to visualise a tranquil scene.

This is torture! she reckoned and wished the flight would end. It seemed to take forever, being on the plane. She needed to use the bathroom; how will I get there if my legs buckle under me, she muttered to herself. Seat holding, she managed the walk to the back of the plane, and somehow got through that ordeal. Wishing the flight would end, she got back to her seat. Her wish was about to be fulfilled. The flight was terminating, at close to midnight and she was feeling exhausted.

Holding tight onto the arms of her seat, she waited for the descent of the plane which started to renew her fears, so it was back to the breathing exercises. Nausea and sweating evident, her heart racing, she closed her eyes, and tried all the manoeuvres she had used on the ascent. It was a little easier the second time around. With a bump the plane's wheels landed on solid ground; she noticed the city lights like fireflies in the night sky. Her legs felt limp and wobbly, thinking, 'how am I going to walk? I can barely stand.' Feeling dizzy she had to sit for a while, but the main thought running through her head was 'I have done it! I have done it!' She somehow managed to hobble out of the plane, and feeling dizzy she made it to the Customs desk, and then onto the baggage carousel.

•••

Her driver was in the Waiting Area, but first she needed to change her dollars into rupees. The hot humid air struck her like a thunderbolt., and weaving her way through the crowds she found a bank and had the necessary money in her hand, making her way to the waiting area, to find her driver standing with a placard in his hand.

'Good evening, madam. Hope you had a good flight?'

'Yes, thank you, as good as it could possibly be, I guess.' Exhausted, she fell asleep in the car until they reached her luxurious hotel by the sea. The reception staff at the hotel were friendly and efficient. She had to show her passport and get her room number. Dazed and tired she made her way to the lift, the room boy in charge of her luggage. Relieved she was now in her own space, and after a quick shower, she fell asleep to the conciliatory sounds of the crashing surf outside her window. This was just the tonic she needed.

•••

The cawing of crows woke her to greet a new day in a new city, in a different country. It was wonderful, and Zelma felt a sense of exhilaration. She was soon to meet the love of her life, and that was exciting. Looking out of her window she drank in the magic of the tropical island. The little native boys playing cricket, the sound of horns blaring, the bright blue ocean with a ship gliding past in the distance. the sun rising over the horizon, and the tall coconut trees etched against the blue sky, with a dark cloud hanging around. As she stared at it, she wondered, *was this an omen? The first dark cloud in the blue of my own sky. Was this going to be a fairy tale ending or a sinister denouement?*

The telephone rang to wake her out of her reverie. Digby calling, 'Hello, my love, welcome. Hope you had a successful trip, and overcame your fears? I'm leaving today to stay in a park bungalow inside the National Park for about three or four nights. We can meet before I start my assignment. I'm sure Tissa will organise something.'

Zelma delighted at hearing him in the same country, 'I'm so looking forward to seeing you again. I had a successful trip and managed to keep my aviophobia under wraps, with some heavy work from Lucy, or so I thought. I'll leave for Puttalam today and see you very soon.'

Zelma had a satisfying buffet breakfast of Eastern and Western delicious food. This being her first overseas trip, it was special. An entirely different culture, a hot and humid climate, an exotic gastronomical experience to one accustomed to simple food. She was due to leave Colombo at mid-morning, with the same driver as on the previous night, for her lagoon and seaside hotel in Puttalam. The air was hot, with fresh sea breezes wafting into her. The blaring of horns on the road outside her hotel, the noise, the dust, piles of garbage left outside buildings with crows pecking at the rubbish, was something she was trying to take in. Signs in her hotel room saying *do not drink water off the tap*, alerted her to the many tropical infections lying around. The very courteous staff impressed her, always waiting on the visitors' every need. All she had to do was sit by the pool and wait to be collected by her driver.

•••

Driving out of Colombo was quicker than expected, being a Sunday. Once on the rural roads, her driver became her tour guide. 'Could you please tell me the sights as we pass them?'

'Of course, madam. We are now passing paddy fields where we get our rice. It is harvesting time, and the farmers do not have machines, so it is all done by hand. The women are cutting the corn. I will stop for a photograph if you like. That is a funeral procession, the young girls wear white clothes, and there is beating of drums, and the girls dance as they walk along.' A delighted Zelma took several photographs.

'Oh look, I must get a photograph of an elephant walking on the road with his mahout by his side,' said an excited Zelma, who alighted from the car and wanted to take heaps of photographs: the mahout asking for payment for his photo being taken, Zelma readily obliged. Then it was onward bound on the narrow road, the car horn blaring non-stop to get some space on the road, in competition with hand driven carts, stray dogs, buses, lorries, the odd rickshaw, tuk tuks, and cattle. All the while Zelma amazed at the sights she was seeing. They passed a large bo-tree under which a small replica of the Lord Buddha sat, the driver bending his head in humility.

They stopped at the Central Colonial Hotel in Chilaw, a small seaside town, for lunch. A delicious rice and mild curry lunch awaited Zelma, who was getting her taste buds acclimatised to an Eastern diet. The hotel was of two storeys with verandas all around with a paddock on one side where a few cattle grazed. The principal room in the hotel had a bar which divided the room into two parts; there was a long low dining room and a small hall with a round table and wicker chairs. The bedrooms, on each side of a central passage at the end of which were two rooms which serve as washrooms. It had a real colonial feel to it and made her imagine how the men of a bygone era had lived.

After lunch they made their way back onwards towards Puttalam, back to the slow progress of a road where speed was only for the fearless, and the intoxicated.

About five pm they arrived at her Puttalam Hotel, situated between a lagoon and the sea. On one side was the calm lagoon where fishermen in small wooden boats were casting their nets to catch lagoon crabs and prawns for the local tourist market.

On the other side was the pounding surf where enormous waves crashed on to the shore, and only surfers would venture out to ride those waves. The lagoon had a bridge made of bent coconut trees laid end to end and supported by a forked branch driven into the bottom of the trees. The locals came to bathe in the lagoon and wash their clothes in the same water, beating them on large rocks to get them sparkling white. This was a whole new experience which fascinated Zelma, and she had to stop and take it all in for a good half hour.

Digby had said he would meet her there, so she phoned him to arrange their brief reunion, which she was so looking forward to.

ELEVEN

PUTTALAM, AND INTO WILPATTU NATIONAL PARK

Digby was preparing to be driven by Palitha together with Sunil and Bandara, from the eastern town of Amparai, to the north-western province for his assignment in the Wilpattu National Park. He was sore from his last melee, but it didn't bother him. He purchased the necessary food supplies at the large town of Anuradhapura, and in two vehicles as before, proceeded to a park bungalow in the national park. The resident cook would take charge of all food supplies, as there would be no watch huts necessary. All poaching monitoring would be done in vehicles, or from the bungalow itself.

Tissa had organised for Zelma to meet Digby at her hotel, and he would stay the night there, before moving on the next morning for the usual 'Cook's tour' of the park, to ascertain its geography and familiarise the team with as much information as they could collect. The days spent alone, were like a jail sentence to Zelma, dark menacing days and even darker nights. She sighed in relief at the thought of being in Digby's arms again. At the hotel she stayed in, the surrounding countryside was undulating, affording spacious views of a long-forgotten lagoon where cormorants dipped their beaks into the water to plunder fish as they scuttled away, then spread their wings on the bank to dry them out.

At seeing him, looking tanned and slightly slimmer, she ran into his arms; the feel of his arms around her holding her so tight was like a strait jacket of yester-year.

'It's wonderful being with you again. I've missed you so much. The sunlight has done wonders for your complexion, my darling.' All Digby could do was kiss her passionately, repeatedly. They were both overjoyed at seeing each other, especially in such a romantic location. After a typical tropical dinner, they took a walk outside in the warm balmy evening. Frangipani, bougainvillea, rhododendrons filled the air with sweet aromas, whilst a house sparrow hopped from leaf to leaf. They both wanted this magic to last forever; this was paradise. Zelma hated the thought of him going back into the jungle; she wanted the night to never end. Words were redundant, they just wanted to be with each other. Going back into their hotel room, the two of them didn't have much to say, holding each other tight was all they wanted.

He undressed her slowly kissing her body all over, in expectant yearning and wonderful fulfilment they lay next to each other. She ran her hand all over his body; they were in glorious synchrony. Rolling around on the bed they both reached orgasm simultaneously. Then fell asleep in each other's arms.

•••

The next morning Palitha the driver collected Digby after breakfast, and they drove into the park after collecting the compulsory tracker Lalith, who would stay with them in the park bungalow. Tissa had given Digby some information on the park, being drier than Yala, with a larger collection of animals and many freshwater lakes surrounded by dense forest. There being two rivers, Digby reasoned that the animals and poachers would congregate around the water, or near the waterhole where a large herd of elephants were already in residence. As walking is not permitted, they must remain in their vehicles, and they decided to stay in their two vehicles close to a water hole strategically placed near the sea, from where poachers would probably arrive. After driving around for a few hours, they returned to their bungalow for a rest before nightfall.

At dusk a lone owl hoots, and a devil bird lets out its eerie and haunting call of a woman being murdered. This was the initiation into the Wilpattu jungle. The team had a light dinner, got into their two vehicles and moved slowly with very dimmed headlights into vantage points under large trees, and waited.

Silence, then footsteps; five men dressed in shorts and short sleeved shirts arrived in a boat, secured it on land, and stealthily tread their way parting the bushes, whispering to each other. They had small torches, carried bows and arrows and two guns. Then another two emerged and join them. They stalked a small deer, but it ran away from them, as they appeared noisy and uncoordinated. They then got together in a huddle and whispered to each other, and then moved on, keeping close to each other. Digby's team sat it out for another hour, but there was no activity, seeming to be a quiet night, they moved back to their bungalow for the rest of the night.

•••

Morning in Kalli Villu was tranquil. It had been a windy night, rattling the aluminium roof of their bungalow, but as dawn broke this silence was broken by the raucous cry of the hornbill, which had made its home in a nearby tree. Like a symphony orchestra, birds began to sing as daylight grew stronger, and another day had dawned in Wilpattu. As the morning sun came out, a large herd of deer led by a magnificent antler, approached warily from the edge of the jungle. Stopping and sniffing the air, they approached the water, and when they felt safe, broke into a run and headed straight for it. Behind came the sound of wild boar, who wallowed in the mud. The buffaloes sat on the opposite shore of the water, calmly chewing their cud; the crocodiles were on the bank waiting for the sun to come out, and as the sun climbed higher only the buffaloes and crocodiles remained. A large bull elephant led a small family group for a drink and a bath in the water, sniffing the air with its trunk turning it from side to side to determine if any human scent could be picked up.

•••

In the evening Digby and his team of seven, now including Anura and Gamini, left at about seven planning to park as on the previous night, under a clump of trees. They noticed fresh leopard pug marks in the sand and mud, and elephant dung down the road, indicating fresh animal presence that day. Lalith spotted three pairs of bare human footprints, fresh from the previous night. Whilst driving they found a dead deer which had been near another villu, with its antlers removed, and some of the flesh cut away. They changed plans and parked near the water tank under a couple of thick bushes and waited. For some reason, the birds were overexcited that night making a commotion, flying everywhere in the night sky.

About an hour later they heard soft footsteps, lit up by small pencil light torches, speaking in undertones, 'Meheta wareng,' ('come this way') the three of them stalking a deer. One of them let fly an arrow which pierced the animal and the deer fell. Then a gunshot rang out, another two shots were fired, all within close range of Digby's men. Birds flew out of trees, squawking loudly.

Digby's team raced out and jumped on the men throwing punches, when out of the bushes another two men arrived. There was pandemonium; in the partial moonlight it was difficult to make out who was on Digby's team, and who were the bellicose poachers. 'Veesige putha, addoo marapiang.' (Prostitute's son; kill them.)

And from the others. 'F…king criminals, kill the bastards. Son of a bitch.'

Sweaty bodies were hard to grip, long hair pulled and yanked, Digby's heart racing, throwing karate kicks some into thin air and some engaging on human body. Thud, boom, groan, crack and squeal heard in the silence of the night. Digby could taste blood in his mouth as he felt a heavy blow to the front of his head, heard a cracking sound, staggered around, and fell to the ground, as did his gun, His head was spinning, and he was losing consciousness. Sunil came up to him and dragged him away. Two poachers lay bleeding on the ground, as was Palitha bleeding and fallen. Anura and Gamini were also trying to fight off their attackers, and in the dark, they had to rely on the fact that the poachers were mostly bare foot, however two poachers ran off. A dying leopard also lay bleeding in the partial moonlight. They turned on the headlights of their vehicles, to take stock of the scene of destruction. The worst causality was Digby, who was bleeding from a head wound, unconscious, and seemed in a bad way. He needed to be taken to a hospital. Palitha too, was bleeding from his chest. The four poachers left behind were handcuffed and bundled into two vehicles, together with Digby and Palitha, and they were taken to Puttalam, half an hour's drive away.

•••

It was midnight when the team arrived, and Digby with Palitha were wheeled into the Emergency Department. Sunil had a fractured leg, and Palitha a chest injury, but Digby was the worst of them all. The poachers in the vehicles were placed under police guard and taken into a special Police Hospital. At the Puttalam Hospital there was a ward with a few beds, filled with sick patients, the single doctor and surgeon on duty were run off their feet trying to attend to the care of an overcrowded hospital. All they could do was set up a fluid drip and monitor his vital signs. A brain x-ray showed bleeding over the front of Digby's brain, which needed immediate surgery; something a small country hospital couldn't provide; he needed a transfer to Colombo. He was muttering incoherently, with vomiting or retching every now and again. Tissa and Zelma were informed of the developments. An intravenous drip was inserted into his arm and an air ambulance organised. The medical team were also assisting in treating the others who were injured, staff stretched to their limits, with a shortage of beds. With no provision for single rooms; a ward held anything from ten to fifteen beds, separated by a curtain or a screen. Many patients could be heard groaning in pain; but, thankfully, Digby was unaware of all that was going on.

Zelma came in immediately she received the news. She arrived to find Digby looking pale, unconscious, and extremely ill. The hospital staff were overwhelmed, a few nurses trying to render treatment to men with multiple injuries, clearly outside their realm of expertise. Bandages, suture material, pain killers and other equipment all required, with little resources to provide it. A tight bandage was put on his bleeding head wound, sufficient to stop the bleeding.

Zelma kept holding Digby's hand, trying to speak to him. 'Digby, my love, can you hear me?' she kept repeating, but got not a flicker of a response.

What if he dies? No, I won't let that happen, she kept repeating to herself, whilst she arranged to travel in the air ambulance with him. Not usually religious, she kept praying that he would survive.

After what seemed an eternity, they arrived at the Colombo Hospital, where he was immediately wheeled along long corridors into the operating theatre. A large hospital, the premier teaching hospital in Colombo was always filled to overflowing with patients. Digby was under the care of the neurosurgeon on duty; he looked very ill, his breathing shallow and slow, pale from blood loss, and mumbling incoherently. Zelma was so afraid he would die before surgery, or on the operating table. Seeing all those white-coated doctors attending to him, she feared the worst. She had to sign the consent for surgery form, as his next of kin. It was all a blur; she mechanically signed the form.

This hospital was much better equipped with numerous staff and doctors to attend to patients. Zelma, a pale, lonely figure, sat outside, or walked up and down along the corridors. Dawn was breaking; Zelma coping with plenty of cups of coffee to keep her awake, and after a few hours in theatre, the operation was completed; Digby wheeled out with oxygen mask over his face, and numerous tubes passing through his veins attached to litres of fluid, to keep him alive. Tissa arrived to witness the tragic state that Digby was in; words could not convey the emotions he was feeling. All Digby's vital signs were beginning to improve, the surgeon met Zelma to tell her the good news, that the blood on Digby's brain had been drained out, that the next forty-eight hours were critical, and they would observe him in the Intensive Care Unit. The hospital was adequately equipped to treat him, not having all the sophisticated equipment that Zelma may have witnessed back in Melbourne, but nevertheless, it sufficient to meet his needs. The doctors and nurses were extremely attentive to him. He was taken into a post-operative ward with five other patients, all recovering from surgery. It was only a curtain screen that separated Digby from the patient next to him, there was a smell of antiseptic in the ward, nauseating, and sterile. From there he was transferred into the special unit for monitoring his recovery. Zelma sat a little away from him waiting for him to come out of the anaesthesia, which in her mind seemed to take ages. Contemplating all the events, saying to herself, *Maybe it's a good omen, he has gone through the worst of it and come out successful.* After what seemed an eternity, he blinked his eyes open and saw her seated next to him, still very groggy, unable to comprehend in any way what was going on around him. Zelma tried to talk to him, but that was futile, he closed his eyes and went back to sleep. All she could do was put her head on the back of her chair and fall asleep, tired and worn out. The ward doctor arrived to monitor his vital signs, seeing Zelma exhausted he advised her to go to her hotel and get some rest, which was pleasing to a young woman, emotionally and physically drained.

•••

Two days later Digby was awake but drowsy, unable to respond to visitors, leaving Zelma to get a well-earned rest in her Colombo hotel. It would be at least two days before he would be alert and coherent, giving Zelma time to contact John and Gladys, as well as Scott and Digby's employer. When she visited him in the ward, she greeted him with a broad smile, to see him lying in bed, looking all around.

'Hello darling, I'm so happy to see you awake and improving. How are you feeling?'

He looked at her with a blank look on his face. 'Where am I, and who are all these people around me? Do I know you? Why am I dressed in these clothes?' Trying to pull off his bandages, becoming mildly boisterous, trying to get off his bed, the nurses sprang into action sedating him, whilst closely monitoring him.

Zelma was astounded! Digby didn't recognise her. What had happened to him? This was hard to comprehend. She had to speak to his surgeon and ward doctor, maybe it was temporary, too soon after surgery, she reasoned.

Doctor Fernando told Zelma, 'Digby has lost his memory, this maybe transient, we must observe him. After head injuries, especially to the front of the brain, memory loss can occur. Let's wait until he has recovered fully from the anaesthesia and the surgery, and we'll assess him then.'

Zelma was in a trance; she couldn't believe what she was hearing and seeing. The love of her life was now a different man, pale from loss of blood, weak from the events of the past few days, and now it seems mentally unwell. She had to speak to his family. She phoned his parents and Gladys answered. 'Hello, Zelma dear, I was expecting a call from you on Digby. How is he?'

Zelma could hardly speak. 'Gladys, please sit down for what I've got to tell you. Digby is in a bad way; he's weak physically, but mentally and emotionally he has totally changed. He received a bad blow to his head in the Wilpattu Park at night, fell unconscious, needed to be airlifted for surgery in Colombo to drain the blood on his brain. He had to spend two days in the Intensive Care Unit, but he can't remember anything of what happened, and most importantly he can't remember me! I'm in a state of shock. His surgeon wants to wait for a few days to see if his memory and recognition will return, as apparently this does happen sometimes.'

Gladys was determined not to allow Zelma to be alone at a time like this.

'Zelma, you can't face this alone. John and I will plan to come out as soon as we can. Hang in there as best as you can,' Gladys tried to share Zelma's anguish.

Zelma very appreciative, and added, 'Thank you Gladys, for coming over with John, who I hope will be able to make the trip in his wheelchair. I'll plan for your arrival and accommodation, just as soon as you can get things organised. Please inform Scott of the developments.'

'John is getting somewhat accustomed to his new predicament; we'll cope. Digby is far more serious. We'll see you as soon as we can. Please organise our hotel, dear.'

•••

Zelma tried visiting Digby again the next day, but there was no change in him. He appeared distressed at the strange woman who spoke to him in endearing terms. It was upsetting, and she didn't know what to do next. She tried to jog his memory, but putting him through any mental stress angered him, even making him more agitated. The worst part of it was that he couldn't even remember his name, or the events leading up to the injury. His mind was a total blank on everything. The doctors decided to move him to the neurosurgical unit.

The next day, in hospital Digby woke to sterile surroundings in a single room. Looking out of the window on the fourth floor, he had a faraway look in his eyes when Zelma walked into the room. He looked perplexed when he saw Zelma, who knew he didn't recognise her. She tried to sit beside him and hold his hand, but he withdrew from her. She tried again to make contact, 'Digby, please try to remember who you are, who I am and what has happened in the past few days. I am your girlfriend from Australia,' she reminded him in a softly spoken voice trying not to show her anguish.

However, he was having none of it. He looked at her blankly, 'I cannot remember having met you before. All girls will want to call me their boyfriend!' A totally changed man now sat before her. A nurse walked in and wanted to check him over, so Zelma had to leave. She was frozen in disbelief! This was all too traumatic for her, so she had to wander away and take a walk in the grounds of the hospital. She couldn't plumb the depths of this conundrum. She sat down under a large tree, listening to the cawing of the crows, and started to cry, wishing that John and Gladys would arrive soon, someone else to share her grief with. She decided to have a talk with his treating doctor who was sympathetic and kind.

'I understand this is difficult for you, Zelma. He isn't the man you last spoke to before his trip into the jungle. The wound on his head must heal, we are closely monitoring his recovery, which could take many weeks or even months. It is a slow process; when he is well enough, he could travel back to Melbourne for further treatment.'

•••

John and Gladys jetted into Colombo at midnight a day later; all accommodation had been organised in the same hotel as Zelma had been staying at. They planned to visit their son alone the next day. After a restful night they visited him in his single room.

'Hello, son,' John greeted him cheerily. Digby responded with a blank stare, but the hint of a faint smile. 'Hope you recognise your mother and I; we have come from Morwell, Australia to see you after Zelma informed us of your injury. How are you feeling today?'

Digby responded, 'I seem to vaguely recall your voice, and am trying to remember who you are. You say you are my father. Well, I can't remember any place called Morwell, did you say? This is my country now – I'm living here, and this is where I want to stay.'

John, trying to jog his son's memory, went on, 'Your name is Digby Trott, and you travelled to Sri Lanka to do conservation work protecting wild elephants, and apprehending poachers. You were attacked along with a couple of others, in a place called Wilpattu. Can you remember any of that?'

Digby continued to have a blank look on his face. 'Can't say I do. Why are all of you pestering me with these questions? I've got a headache trying to remember anything.'

John decided it was better to leave things alone for the time being and talk about Digby's present situation. 'How are you getting on here in this hospital, and are you sleeping alright, eating alright?' Digby sat up on his bed, clearly more comfortable to talk about his present hospital stay.

'Well, I like it here, the people here are kind and I feel I'm well looked after.'

His doctor walked in and was happy to meet John and Gladys. Happy to answer any questions they put to him, if the talk focused on Digby's present situation, and not his future.

The doctor was sympathetic to their dilemma, 'Digby will take some time to recover, and I ask if you could just talk to him as calmly as possible, so as not to upset him,' he told them after calling them aside. John wanted to ask further questions, but they were deferred.

After a while it looked like Digby was tiring, and they left to get some rest themselves and recover from jet lag after a long flight.

•••

The next day Tissa arrived hoping to meet Digby, who was sitting up in bed looking perplexed at all that was going on around him. 'Hello Digby, nice to see you again, after all you have been through.'

'I don't believe I know who you are. Where and when have I met you?' Digby replied, looking uninterested.

'We pursued poachers in the jungles, and you were attacked. I intend to deal severely with the ones we caught and are now in custody. They are responsible for your injuries.'

Digby looked away, showing no interest. 'No, I remember nothing, although I want to.'

Tissa could only shake his head in amazement, looking at a visibly lean man, so different to the man who had started out a few weeks ago. Realising that pursuing conversation was futile, he shook Digby's hand and left the ward, vowing to severely punish the nefarious criminals and find the bosses of the crime syndicates. There was a conference scheduled in the ward to decide on the next course of action in rehabilitation, involving Zelma, John and Gladys and Tissa if he wanted to attend. As it was still only a week since the injury, and his wounds were healing, the doctors decided he was too unwell to travel. He needed to see more health professionals who would try to jog his memory and do as much as was possible with the limited resources available in Colombo, and the plan was to transfer care to Australia later. A neuropsychologist was assigned to his treating team to perform tests and therapy for two weeks. Zelma who found she was not progressing with recognition from Digby's perspective, decided she would return to Melbourne as her leave had run out, it being too upsetting seeing him in the state he was in.

Entering his room she greeted him with a handshake on this occasion, churning up inside at the difference in him. 'I'll be leaving for Melbourne tomorrow, Digby; I will keep in touch with your parents as to your progress, and will see you in Melbourne when you return,' she said, trying to hide the tears in her eyes and the pain in her voice. All she received from him was a vacant stare, perhaps the faint glimmer of a smile. She had to face the prospect of returning on a plane alone and had some lingering doubts regarding controlling her panic attacks, but felt having done it once, the second time around would be easier. She bought her ticket and boarded a direct flight, went through all the steps she had taken on her flight into Colombo, and was feeling a little less pressured and slightly more confident.

TWELVE

RETURN TO MELBOURNE A CHANGED MAN

'Digby, I want you to try and decipher a puzzle of varying shapes,and tell me what you see there.' The psychologist had set up a test and questioned him.

'I see two faces, maybe not. Perhaps it is a bird. I don't know! This is too demanding. I hate these tests.'

Progress in Colombo was slow. John and Gladys decided that it was, perhaps time to transfer him back home, as he was walking around feeling well, and gaining weight, but psychologically, no progress was being made. He was still confused and unable to concentrate on any topic for long periods. If he were pushed to try any tasks he would erupt in anger.

Tissa arrived to say goodbye, 'I don't suppose you remember me? Tissa, who organised your trip? Nevertheless, I'll keep in contact with the treating team and your family. I do hope you will recover in the not-too-distant future, and we can renew our friendship.'

'Thank you. I'll do my best to recover. I want to remember.'

The airfares were organised, the Melbourne treating doctors contacted, and arrangements made for his transfer. On the plane he was assigned a seat in the middle row, between John and Gladys. His Colombo neurosurgeon who was contacted said to the treating doctors, he was hopeful Digby would recover, as he believed his frontal lobe injury was temporary, but he couldn't specify a time frame.

•••

Monday morning at the seafront hotel where the Trott's were staying turned out to be a sunny day. After a hearty breakfast, they collected their son from the hospital and proceeded to the airport. Digby was confused as to where he was going, and why he needed to get on a plane.

'Where are we heading, and why do I need to get on a plane? This is my home now, and I want to stay here. I don't remember living anywhere else,' he protested loudly in a plaintive voice.

Almost kicking and screaming he was put into a taxi, only feeble John being able to placate him to a certain extent. The doctors had given Digby some sedating mixture before he left, quietening him down somewhat. After an hour's drive they arrived at a crowded airport, John looking in despair at the crowds, and hoping he wouldn't lose his son if he tried to run off. Fortunately, the medication was working, and they managed to get through the formalities both as wheelchair passengers, before arriving at their boarding gate, Digby clearly almost nodding off to sleep. Relieved he would not be an embarrassment they sat in the waiting area. On the plane he was seated comfortably between his parents, almost asleep, to everyone's relief. He was slowly coming round to the fact that these were his parents, as they both kept reminding him of childhood activities, which he seemed interested to hear. Still protesting the need to be travelling from what he considered his home to another place, he believed he was the victim of a conspiracy, and sat with a saturnine countenance throughout the trip. 'I don't believe you are telling me the truth,' he repeatedly protested.

•••

Back at Tullamarine Airport on a warm spring day the flight from Colombo taxied to a halt.

Digby showed no recognition of the airport, or the familiar Australian accents around him. However, he offered no resistance to being taken through the usual formalities, and then onto the baggage carousel. They caught a taxi to get to Digby's apartment in the city where his parents would stay whilst his treatment was being formalised.

'Where are we going?' Digby impatiently asked, but his weary parents were in no mood to answer him. Arriving at his apartment, he showed no recognition of the small apartment with his clothes lying strewn everywhere, just following John into his bedroom. Exhausted they all fell asleep.

•••

The next day, Digby, John and Gladys, arrived for his assessment at the Melbourne hospital, Zelma being there as well to provide her input. The examining doctor greeted Digby, 'Hello,' and shook his hand, inviting them all to sit down 'Do you know what brings you here?' he looked at Digby.

'No, I'm just doing what I was told to do, and don't see anything wrong with me, and I do want to return to where I came from. My head aches and I want to try and remember things that are supposed to have happened in the jungles; that's what I've been told.'

Then Digby became overexcited and wanted to leave the room, protesting he was being held against his will. It was obvious that the assessment would have to be done in stages, with a largely uncooperative Digby. The doctor decided that admission would be necessary. So, Digby was sedated, when, hopefully, he would later become cooperative so that details of the injury and the treatment would become clearer. With that decision made, they all returned to their homes, Digby unable to recognise Zelma once again.

The next day John and Gladys made the trip to hospital, this time to admit Digby into a private room, hoping he would not run off. With the necessary sedation, he became more cooperative; John decided he would return to the farm, and Gladys would stay in Melbourne, visit her son when required and return with him later.

In hospital, he was quizzed once more. 'Good morning, Digby, do you recall any part of your life before you came into hospital, and do you know where you are now?' the kindly doctor tried again.

'I have been told my name is Digby Trott, that I was born overseas, and I had an injury to my head where there now is a large scar. I'm unable to tell you anything else, 'cos I can't remember what happened to me. All I know is that I've got a large wound on my head, and sometimes I get headaches. I'd like to remember more.' Sitting there yawning and showing no interest in the questions, the interview was terminated. The next day after gentle questioning from a psychologist, he said he could vaguely remember his university days, but not much of his school days, and hardly anything of his early life in Sri Lanka. Some pictures were produced from Gladys, but that didn't stir his memory. A picture of Scott from his school days was shown to him.

'I sort of seem to remember that face. Who is he? Someone I know well?" Digby responded.

This was encouraging to the treatment team, some slight glimmer of hope. A clinical hypnotist was the next step, and someone was assigned to test his memory under hypnosis just in case he was malingering. The next day, after getting the appropriate medication which put him into a trance-like state, he was again questioned, as before and he came up with the same answers. 'I do sort of recall boarding a plane and arriving at an airport, and going to my apartment, which I'm told I've been renting. I'm told I suffered an injury in the jungles but can't remember any of that.'

They decided to let him stay for more tests done at a slow pace, as he was becoming confused and irascible, and needed to have his mental pain alleviated.

Gladys decided he needed to be cared for on the farm when all his tests were completed, including brain scans, and she would remain at his apartment taking him home with her, and contacting his employer about his work and leave without pay if available. If not, he would resign from his employment until he was hopefully cured. In any case Gladys decided he would relinquish his rental apartment; the budget was getting too tight to keep it going.

•••

Zelma loved Digby, and was prepared to endure watchful waiting, hoping he would recover. She visited him on the ward, greeting him tentatively, with a smile, 'Hello Digby,' said quietly, waiting for any sign of recognition, looking as lovely as ever and wearing the perfume he had loved. He stared at her as if transfixed, that such a beautiful woman would visit him. She went on, 'I'm Zelma, your girlfriend, who was with you in Sri Lanka when you had that awful hit to your head,' said in a subdued voice, hoping he would remember something.

'I would love to believe you if only I could remember. That perfume you're wearing seems to remind me of something. Please keep talking and remind me, I want to remember who you are.'

'Well, we met at a pub and went out together on many occasions, you met my family, and I met your parents at their farm in a place called Morwell. We had been going out together for months. I will come by everyday whilst you are here, if you want me to, just to keep reminding you of what we had together,' kissing him lightly on the cheek. Digby was too transfixed to speak, amazed that he knew such a pretty girl, who would hang around for him. She sat on his bed, but he appeared uncomfortable, so she sat on a chair in the room. He had a confused look on his face and looked worried.

'I feel you are trying, Digby, and I hope you want us to be back together again, but I won't push you. Let the doctors and treatments take their time. However, I can't wait forever, and I want you to try and remember. It's hard being rejected by you.' She was hurting inside and found his rejections hard to take.

'Please sit down. Did you say your name was Zelma? I'm trying to remember you. Please give me some time.' Digby sat up and looked intently at Zelma.

He was in the ward for a few more days with memory recovery therapy given to jog his brain, and Zelma lovingly visited daily hoping to help in his recovery, but progress was extremely slow, and his memory kept failing him, even though he wanted to remember the past. Investigations came back inconclusive, leaving Gladys to take him with her to Morwell, and let the treatment plan take a break from the hospital. Perhaps, going back to familiar territory would be helpful, was the opinion of the doctor on the ward.

•••

In Gippsland Scott was soldering on, pursuing Jack, whenever he had some time off work. Knowledge of his favourite pubs, and travel haunts narrowed the area of surveillance, and he figured that in small or large country towns trying to locate somebody would be easier than in large cities. He did know that Jack had charm, but never learnt from experience, was easily influenced and suggestible, and could be at the mercy of unscrupulous people. Maybe he had joined a philanthropically supported colony somewhere in the bush, where he would be exceedingly difficult to find. Cruising around his usual haunts Scott did finally stumble on Jack drinking with some of his buddies, in a cottage just outside Morwell. As usual he was inebriated with slurred speech.

'Hello Jack, do you remember me?' Scott asked nonchalantly. 'I first met you at Traralgon Airport after the fire, I met you with Digby and we had lunch together, the three of us.'

'Don't remember you. Maybe you're the person I was with last night at the game of cards, at the pub?' Jack responded glibly, looking at Scott with a blank look on his face.

Just then a group of unkempt looking inimical youths gathered around looking mean and vengeful, 'Leave him alone or we'll thump you,' a particularly nasty looking man barked at Scott.

Scott backed off not wanting any trouble with drunks. If Jack was innocent of the airport tower fire, then Scott would like to save him from a world of wasted opportunities, but first he had to get him away from his group of no-good so-called friends. He decided to go and collect Betty Smith who lived nearby. Maybe she could lure Jack to live with her for a while.

Scott drove up to Betty's house, who was surprised to see Scott looking rather flustered. 'Betty, I need your assistance to help me rescue your wandering nephew from himself and his mates. He is drunk, and in the company of young men, who are not helpful to him. They are all drunk and creating an awful ruckus at a house nearby. Betty grabbed her coat, and together they drove back to where Jack was squatting with his friends. As Betty seemed to have a good influence on him; Jack meekly agreed to return to Betty's house, together with Scott.

The next day Scott returned to speak to a sober Jack and learned that he had gotten himself into a legion of scrapes and near misses with the police, the best they could do for Jack was to place him in a supervised hostel, where under social worker guidance he could be trained at acquiring some type of job skills. Betty would be informed of his progress. It was a huge undertaking. Scott and Betty were unsure whether it would be successful. Jack's dogs had to be cared for, hopeful that foster homes for them could be found. Eventually a suitable hostel was located, and Jack grudgingly enrolled in their treatment plans, whilst his dogs went to good homes for a holiday.

Jack was taught socialising skills, budgeting skills and anger management training, and whilst living with others; he was gradually able to try and integrate into a rural community. Betty was pleased with Jack's progress, and soon he was able to obtain work as a labourer, continuing to live in the hostel until he was less gauche in himself, claiming he would still like to join his friends on the weekends. It was hoped he didn't smoke weed and if he did, he kept that well disguised. Alcohol indulgence was a long-term problem for now, anyway.

'Let's give things some time,' Betty remarked hopefully. 'A few bad habits might be difficult to break, meeting his friends now and again can be allowed. Only time will tell.'

•••

Digby moved his belongings into his parent's Morwell farmhouse and settled into an indolent lifestyle much to the disappointment of John and Gladys. Helping with chores around the farm was anathema to him, and requests to help were met with annoyance. He did as he pleased, leaving home whenever he felt like it, being rude to his parents, now a norm for him.

'I have to go out tonight as I'm meeting some friends at the Morwell Hotel,' he called out to his parents and drove off to the pub not too far away from his home. He returned home in an intoxicated state with a mate who had accompanied him back, saying,

'Digby was not too popular as he was making lewd remarks and loud catcalls.'

'Don't patronize me, I wasn't drunk, and reckon I was very mannerly. I reckon there were too many loud mouths in the pub tonight, it didn't include me,' was his reply, having no idea of how badly he was behaving, and now was a social misfit.

John was extremely distressed to see his son so inebriated, and watch him sink into such depths, correcting him loudly for such a rude reply, but Digby was too drunk to take in any form of chastising, and fell asleep on the couch.

•••

The next morning there was a knock on the door, and Jack Smith introduced himself to Digby. Jack, now working with a local builder, was keeping out of trouble whilst living with Betty. Digby showed no sign of recognition. 'Hello mate, heard you were in town, and I reckon we could catch up over a coffee.'

'Yes, we could if I knew who you were!' Digby responded haughtily.

'You were with Scott when you met me many months ago after the fire at Traralgon Airport and gave me some cash to give you my life history. Remember?'

'Ha ha, can't say that I did, so what?' Digby retaliated. 'Yes, let's go out for a yada, your car or mine?'

'I think I'll drive, get your gear on,' said Jack, waving to Gladys.

'Please take good care of him,' implored Gladys as they walked out the door.

They ended up at a small coffee shop in town, and Jack noticed Digby becoming agitated and restless, not wanting to sit still, so he called Scott. Being a Saturday Scott was at home and said he would join them at the coffee shop. Half an hour later Scott turned up. Seeing Digby after a considerable time and after his accident, he went up to him and put his arms around him attempting to give him a bear hug. Digby would have none of it, pushing him away. Scott was completely taken by surprise to see the change in his best mate. The sloppy clothes, the unshaven face, the sleepy look in his eyes, the loud indignant voice, the transformation was unbelievable.

'Who are you and why do you try to asphyxiate me?' said a bewildered Digby.

Scott looked at him in amazement. He wasn't sure what to say, deciding that the least said was the better, as Digby could so easily respond in anger. Digby surveyed Scott intently, a glimmer of recognition in the depths of his memory.

'I don't remember who either of you are, or what you have to do with me? I can't say I have met either of you before. Perhaps you had better fill me in.'

Scott patiently and calmly reminded Digby,

'Well, we were school friends and best mates at high school, played footy together, have been mates ever since, and worked piloting light planes doing crop dusting and tourist rides on the weekends. Do you remember anything of all that, even a small fragment?'

Digby looked hard at Scott, not sure what to make of the situation, and his story.

'I'd like to believe you if I can remember what you say. Maybe we could take a trip to our so-called secondary school, and a trip to the airport. There are so many parts of my life, in fact most of it, that I can't remember, but I do so want to remember them. I feel a headache coming on now and would like to go back home.'

They agreed, trying to talk to Digby was like hitting their heads on a brick wall. He was so off the conversation, and couldn't stay on one topic, that even Jack found it difficult to understand him. Scott drove Digby home eager to meet John and Gladys and find out what they had to say about the situation.

Knocking on their door Gladys greeted Scott standing there with her son. 'Hello Scott, so nice of you to bring Digby home, I'm glad you two have reconnected.'

'Gladys, maybe we need to talk, together with John, got any time now? How have things gone along since you collected Digby after his accident and since he returned home? I see that he can't remember me, I'm so upset to realise this.'

Digby walked off into his room, not keen to be in on the conversation.

Gladys looked appealingly at Scott. 'We are trying to get our heads around this new version of Digby. He is rude, uninterested, arrogant, vague and disinhibited, so different to the man who left on his adventurous trip. He drives off, not telling us where he's going, and often has his phone turned off so we can't trace him. Any help from you would be wonderful. Why not stay for lunch, just a hamburger meal?'

This meal was going to be an ordeal of its own making.

Sitting down to lunch Scott was upset to see the anguish and pain on the faces of John and Gladys.

'Scott, what did you say we did at school? I think I might have been the class clown, getting into numerous pranks with the teachers, and leading you on. I think I had so many girlfriends I couldn't count them on the fingers of two hands. What say you and I go look for some of those girls we dated, maybe we can go tonight?' Digby said tapping his fingers on the dining table.

'No, I'm sorry to disappoint you, Digby, we played plenty of sport at school, you became a gym junkie, and a karate black belt, girls were not on our agenda,' Scott replied trying to sound as imperturbable as he could in order to plumb the depths of this new enigma that was Digby.

John and Gladys were taking all this in; Gladys with tears welling up in her eyes. Digby was going off the rails. She had to contact his treating team in Melbourne and inform them of this new whimsical son of hers.

They were all glad when the meal was over, Scott promising to come over when he could and take Digby out to see his old school, and the Traralgon Airport to help jog his memory. John wheeling along, and Gladys went out to tend their animals, and Digby retreated into his room.

The next day Gladys contacted his treating doctor to update him on the recent events in Digby's life and scheduled a visit to Melbourne for a review. He gave Digby a new appointment but warned Gladys that it was a long road back, and some new medication could be trialled if the family agreed, especially Digby, who until now had resisted any new medication.

• • •

Digby tried helping around the farm, but his lack of initiative, spontaneity, and poor concentration didn't help his cause; in frustration at being unable to prove himself of much use he threw his tools down and wandered off outside the gate. Gladys, concerned that Digby might wander away, got into the family utility to collect him, bringing him home, and left him to rest, rather than force him to work.

That evening Digby decided he would have a night out on the town, got into his car calling out to his father, 'Dad, I have a date in town this evening and will be taking my car. I hope to be at the pub,' he announced in a glib manner and without waiting for a reply drove off. His exasperated father grumbling under his breath at how much his son had changed.

Playing loud music, with screeching tyres, he drove into the night, having regressed into a teenager again. Arriving at the pub Digby got stuck into the beer, when Jack arrived, greeting him warmly. 'I've got a date with a lady here tonight and am waiting to meet her.'

'Oh, do you know her name, and where did you find her?' Jack asked in bewilderment.

'None of your business! Why don't you just bugger off and leave me in peace,' Digby replied in a loud voice, letting all the other patrons know what he was saying.

Even for a man like Jack who was accustomed to harsh, foul words this was difficult to take.

Digby walked up to a group of three women drinking at a table and sat down next to them. 'Hello beautiful,' he said to one of them, 'would you like to come out with me tonight?' She walked away in disgust, and so did her friends, leaving him alone with his beer; yet he didn't realise this was socially and ignominiously inappropriate. He was imbibing alcohol at too fast a rate, being in no condition to drive home, so the friendly barman took him upstairs to a room and allowed him to fall asleep on a bed there. At midnight John and Gladys who were frantic with worry, being unable to reach him on his phone, turned up at the pub, relieved to find him asleep. The barman walked him downstairs and they took him home. As this seemed to be a pattern – he was now developing a love of the amber stuff – they pleaded with Scott to help.

Scott was planning to enlist Jack's help, and together they had to devise a strategy. He arrived at the Trott family farm on his day off from work extremely concerned at Digby's erratic and audacious behaviour.

'Digby, we are all concerned at the things you are doing now. Wandering off or driving away with no clear plan as to where you're going. Do you or don't you want to regain all that you lost, especially your memory?' Scott said looking straight into Digby's eyes.

'I would like to cooperate. Yes, I would like to regain my past, but how do I do it? I seem to have good and bad days, which is something I have no control over.'

Scott spoke to Digby trying to gain his confidence, but as Digby still had no clear recollection of Scott he was disinclined to cooperate, although he didn't acknowledge that there was anything wrong with him; it was only second-hand information from others telling him so.

As planned, Scott collected Digby to take him to their secondary school and then onto the airport. Driving into their High school, he first took him to the football grounds, where Digby took a long look at the playing field, and then the spectator benches. A flicker of recognition crossed his face…perhaps! They walked around the school, all the classrooms were shut, and they could only peer into the classrooms through the windows. Next, they drove to the airport, a small rural one with light aircraft parked in the hangers. The burnt-out air traffic control tower visible, waiting to be demolished; a new one built nearby.

Digby looked long and hard at the airport runways and the planes, 'I seem to recall something in the depths of my mind of this place. That burnt watch tower, yes, I'm seeing something there, you said it was on fire.' An aeroplane was coming into land, and Digby stared intently at it for a few minutes, but didn't say much.

From there the twosome went into town for a beer and a chat, Scott trying to help Digby recall former events. 'Tell me, did any of the places we visited today remind you of anything from your past?' Scott enquired. 'We all want you to recover your memory and get back to the person you were before the accident.'

Digby responded, 'I could if my brain will respond to what I want it to do, but right now I've got truly little recall of my life before the accident. You must believe me, I'm trying. Remind me of the things we got into at school, our love for aeroplanes; that must have come from somewhere.'

'Maybe you may recall the model aeroplane class we attended. We had so much fun building planes, the Lego and Meccano sets we tinkered with for hours. I'm sure it's in the depths of your mind somewhere; it'll come forth sooner or later.' Scott was trying all the ideas he had of restoring his mate's memory.

THIRTEEN

TARRABULGA NATIONAL PARK

Digby woke up one morning with a great yearning for adventure; he donned his hiking boots and his warm gear, packed food and water into his backpack and set off without informing his parents. He didn't have any money on him, so decided to hitchhike along the main road, being fortunate when a truck driver stopped. 'G'day mate, where are you headed.?' a cheery voice called out from the cabin. 'I'm Brett.'

'Just down the highway a short drive from here,' Digby replied and hopped in next to the dog on the seat. 'My name's Digby. I guess I have a sudden yearning to go places today and will start off with a national park I seem to remember is some place around here.'

'Tara Bulga National Park. That's fine, I'm going that way. I'll drop you off. Good day for hiking mate.'

'Nothing to do with the weather gods, I just want to keep truckin' and listen to the birds. It reminds me of places I've been to before, much like women I've known before!'

Brett thought that an unusual remark to hear but ignored it and kept chatting about the weather instead. 'Okay mate, here we are, the entrance is just down the road.'

'Thanks mate, have a good day,' Digby cheerfully replied.

He took a leisurely walk into the park and met an ascetic in a lonely cave, who didn't seem to hear Digby as he was in a trance and wasn't aware of Digby trying to connect with him. The little old man had long straight grey hair and looked weather beaten and frail. He wore old shabby clothes, and his hands were knotted and gnarled. Digby kept on walking deep into the park when a kangaroo jumped out in front of him, causing him to fall in fright.

'What the hell was that?' he screamed, before he realised what it was. He seemed to have hurt his ankle, and found it difficult walking, and sat in the shade of large tree. Ferns reached high into the sky, the smaller ferns being dwarfed by the larger trees. Sunlight was filtering through the leaves shining down on all the splendour of the magnificent forest. He sat down to have some food and noticed that his phone was turned off, so turned it back on, realising his parents must be out looking for him.

Indeed, John and Gladys, when they found him missing, and unable to make contact, became extremely worried, especially as he hadn't taken his car, and his car keys were lying on the kitchen table. They decided to call the police who sent out a patrol van to search for him.

Realising he had no phone reception, and afraid he'd have to spend the night alone in the cold park, he decided to hobble his way along a path hoping it would lead him out and not deeper into the forest. Then he heard trucks and traffic. Even in his confused state he knew he must be close to the highway and hobbled his way forward towards the sound. It was almost nightfall when he landed on the road, exhausted and confused. A police car stopped to identify him and return him to his grateful but angry parents.

John was livid and screamed at Digby, 'Where the hell have you been? We have been sick with worry as to what had happened to you. The police force have other things to do, rather than go looking for an irresponsible young man!'

'If that is how you feel I'll go out again, right now,' Digby screamed back.

Gladys, once more came to the rescue, placating them. 'No need for frayed tempers, let's just sit down to a meal and relax.' She was imploring, 'Digby, I think you owe us an apology.'

'Oh alright. I do apologise,' he said grudgingly.

The evening was spent in quiet television viewing, nobody wanting to talk about the day's activities.

•••

Scott visited the next day to find a sore and weary Digby who was still asleep at midday. The two of them sat in stony silence, Scott trying to work out the gross descent into the pits of social decline Digby had fallen into, whilst trying to plumb the depths of this enigma. Scott was aware it wasn't his wilful acts, but the behaviour of a brain injured man. He had to be taken to Melbourne for the treating team to update his plan of management. Anything was worth a try.

'Digby, I would strongly recommend that you return to Melbourne to ask the doctors to try out some new medication on you, I'm aware that you don't want any tablets, there may be other avenues of treatment. Don't you see that what you did yesterday was wrong, your parents were extremely concerned, and the police were out searching for you. We all want to see you return to your former self; you're young and have your whole life ahead of you.'

It may have been that Scott was overbearing on him, or that Digby was plain uninterested in what the others around him had to say.

Realising he was not getting through to Digby, Scott decided to involve Zelma in his pleadings. After updating her on the status quo, she rang Digby, trying to convince him to come to Melbourne for further tests and treatment.

Digby was not sure who Zelma was and was trying to dig deep into his mind to try and remember her. She phoned him asking if he would oblige, and he seemed half interested in pleasing her, but wouldn't do it for Scott.

He was still not sure who Zelma was. 'Hello, did you say you are Zelma? I seem to recognise your voice somewhere in the back of my mind. What do you want me to come down to Melbourne for? Scott echoes the same thing.'

'Well, maybe we can visit the beachfront restaurant you and I visited some time ago and have a conversation. Scott says he will organise your transport, drop you off at my place, and take you back in the evening.'

'Alright, I'll give it a try. I must say I sort of remember your voice, yet can't quite remember who you are, and don't remember any beachside restaurant. I will contact Scott to tee things up with you.' Digby now seemed genuinely keen to regain his memory.

●●●

The next weekend Scott together with Digby left for Melbourne; on the road whilst stopping at the lights, a couple of good-looking girls walked past. Digby didn't hesitate to put his window down and give them a wolf whistle, leaving Scott very embarrassed.

'What did you do that for?' Scott demanded to know.

'They looked swell and needed to know it. I don't see anything wrong with that!' retorted Digby, showing no sign of recognising socially inappropriate codes of conduct.

'Well, while I'm driving you around could you please be more respectful.' Digby withdrew into a sullen silence.

Scott dropped off Digby at Zelma's apartment. Knocking on her door, he showed a nonchalant attitude to the encounter. Zelma opened the door with a cheery greeting, attempting to give him a kiss on his cheek; he drew back in surprise, no sign of recognition on his face. They stood looking at each other intently, before he stepped into her apartment, which he had known so intimately, if only he could plunge into the depths of his mind.

Zelma was shocked to see him poorly dressed and down at heel. His hair had grown long, and he hadn't bothered to have it cut, his shirt crumpled, with no jacket over it; he had on an old pair of jeans and wore shabby sneakers, not at all sharply dressed as when they went out on their previous dates. Zelma in comparison had on a stylish outfit and perfect makeup. She tried hard not to show her surprise at his social decline, instead focussing on trying to get into rapport with him.

'Let's go then,' she said smiling, and led the way to her car.

Arriving at the restaurant she looked for a glimmer of recognition from him of the place they had visited so many times before, and a feeling of deja vu on his part, but it was not apparent.

'Do you remember this place?' she asked looking intently at his face.

'Not really. Am I supposed to know this place?' Digby replied staring out to the sea from the upper storey window. 'I'd like to remember, as it seems a romantic place to have a meal.'

After they had ordered their usual favourite meal, Zelma thought the time was right to broach the all-important question.

'I would like to ask of you one especially important request. Would you please consider going back into hospital for more tests and treatment, so that you and all of us can look forward to your recovery?' she asked in a plaintive, pleading voice.

He thought for a while, gave a half smile and said, 'Yes, I trust you, and will go back into hospital.'

Zelma was over the moon, telling him how much she admired him for taking that decision. They completed their meal in an amiable manner, no signs of mistrust on his part. Returning to her apartment, she phoned Scott with the good news; he arrived soon afterwards to take Digby back to Morwell. She wanted to put her arms around him and tell him how much she loved him, but she knew she was rushing him, and he would not have believed her, or even remembered her, his memory far too erratic and patchy.

Having returned to the farm, Digby was trying to relive the events of the weekend. He had a liking for Zelma and was trying to remember her from his past. She was beautiful, and if all she told him was factual, he would indeed have been privileged to have her as his girlfriend. She appeared caring and wanted him to recover, although he wasn't convinced that there was anything wrong with him.

•••

Jack Smith was quietly tending his garden and waking early five days a week to start work helping builders with their manual work. He continued to drink on weekends, but Betty reckoned if he kept out of trouble in other ways, he could be allowed one or two faults. He was even saving a little money now and again and had come a long way with his social graces and his appearance.

Scott hoped that a little of Jack's improvement would rub off onto Digby, deciding that the two of them should get together more often.

He spoke to Jack, 'Mate, I'd like you to get together with Digby now and again, and try to teach him social graces, how to dress better, and generally fit in with everyone else. I'll tell him that you will contact him and get together with him, maybe at the footy, on a Saturday afternoon. Would you be able to do that with him?'

'No worries, Scott, happy to help in any way,' Jack responded.

Following up on that Scott phoned Digby. 'Digby, Scott here. You may or may not remember Jack, who you and I met at the Traralgon Airport after the fire in the watch tower. Well, he lives in Morwell and will be contacting you shortly to take you to a local footy match. I'd like you to accept his invitation to go out with him… okay?'

'Scott, I don't remember him or remember a fire at that airport, but I do want to put together all the gaps in my life, so, yes, I'll go along with your plan.'

Jack phoned Gladys rather than Digby to tee up an evening with her son and arrived at one pm on a Saturday. Digby was untidily dressed in dirty faded jeans, a loose soiled jumper and sneakers.

'Oh hello, what's your name, welcome to the house of many moons, ha ha. Where are we off to today?' Digby was swaying and slurring in his speech, quite unconcerned at the effect it had on Jack.

Gladys came out to greet Jack, chastising Digby, 'That is no way to greet Jack, who has given up a day of his weekend to take you out. Those clothes need changing, please do so and be polite to Jack.'

'But I'm the king of the county and can do no wrong.' He was clearly having a bad day. Hadn't slept well, was distracted and apathetic, and might prove more than Jack could handle, but Jack was prepared to give it a try.

'Let's go then. I have my car. It isn't too flash but will get us into town.'

They left driving towards the football ground in town for the start of a match. Digby got out of the car and headed towards the match and the clubhouse. He let out a two-finger whistle and screamed out, 'C'arn the Parrots' distracting all around him. From there he proceeded to the bar, ordered a pint of beer, and put it on John's account. It didn't take long for Jack to join him in his beer drinking. The two of them were becoming increasingly loud and boisterous, requiring a club official to intervene and ask them to leave. Singing loudly, they both left the bar, one as drunk as the other. Digby decided he needed to attend the bathroom but found it more convenient to use the corner of the building as an outside toilet; even Jack in his inebriated state knew this was socially inappropriate. The two of them stumbled into the car park and fell asleep in Jack's car, to the relief of all around them. They woke up hours later, when the sun was setting and headed back to the Trott farm, this outing being a disaster for Digby.

FURTHER TREATMENT

The following Monday he returned to Melbourne for treatment, together with Gladys and John, for further tests and treatment in the brain trauma unit, his saturnine countenance indicating the trauma inside his head. Somehow, he appeared to prefer the disinhibited person he had become. Trying to remember his behaviour on a day-to-day basis was a feat in itself – he could barely remember the events of the previous day.

Walking in the doctor greeted him, 'Hello, Digby. Glad to see you back. Make yourself comfortable in the single room we have for you, and we can proceed with further tests.'

'Okay, doc, whatever you say, the clouds have a silver lining. I don't quite remember why I'm here, thank you none the less.'

The doctor smiled and waited for him to settle down. He would need a full work up. His over-talkativeness was disturbing other patients, and he was being shunned by some of them, making him more tactless and meddlesome.

More scans of his brain came up negative, his intelligence tests were normal, although he was unable to perform complicated activities, or translate complex verbal instructions into motor activity. The consensus of medical opinion was that all tests were not yielding any diagnosis, and that the frontal part of his brain had been shaken up and was slow to recover.

The treating team then met Digby, Gladys and John to give them their opinion. 'We have looked at all the tests and can't find any visible damage to Digby's brain. We suggest that the best treatment is for Digby to return to the scene of the crime and retrace his steps to awaken his brain and reignite his behaviour of old. Taking medication isn't going to help him, and he tells us he will not take tablets anyway.'

Gladys and John couldn't believe what they were hearing. Could this doctor be serious? Take Digby back to the scene of the crime! This was an incredible and ridiculous suggestion, in John's mind.

'We must think about this,' John said in amazement. Digby was silent. Did he want to go back?

He couldn't relate to all that was said. He now decided Morwell was his home and had quite forgotten that he had declared the jungle his home.

'Well, I'm glad I don't need to swallow any more tablets; but what is the scene of the crime? I don't believe any crime was committed. I sort of recall trying to catch poachers and that is what I want to do.'

He believed he was quite normal. They left the ward in a sombre mood for the drive home disheartened. Neither wanted to discuss the suggestion with Digby on the way home.

John and Gladys were stunned with the news. 'I cannot believe that those learned doctors want us to take Digby back to the jungles. They believe that he must retrace his steps to jolt his memory! How on earth can that happen?'

'I believe that he has an underlying love of the jungle and having lost the wildlife and not having fully apprehended the poachers, he may actually enjoy going back, although he doesn't know it now,' Gladys suggested, hoping that was the best thing to do.

John was unconvinced. In the meantime, there was a farm to attend to, and John and Gladys with advancing years already had their work cut out for them. They didn't need an amnesic son to complicate matters.

Returning home, they were both exasperated at all the goings on. He didn't particularly want to travel back to a hot country to try out something that may not work. He shouted out to Digby, taking out his frustrations on him, 'What the hell are you doing now, just lazing around? We need some help around here. This is not a hotel!'

Digby immediately got into his car and drove off, tyres screeching, in a blaze of dust.

It was up to Gladys to soothe things out. They had to discuss the proposal; Gladys prepared to try out anything; but John was not at all convinced. The expenses would have to be negotiated, maybe the American Wildlife Association would cover the costs. John rang Scott to negotiate Digby's possible return with Tissa.

•••

'Tissa, I haven't met you. I'm Digby's best mate. The Melbourne doctors want Digby to return to the scene of the crime in Sri Lanka, to the same wildlife parks he was working in before, to carry out the same activities as on his first trip, but not stay in the watch huts, and they think that will reignite his memory. The stress of apprehending the poachers would not be in it this time.

Can you please organise the accommodation, and the cost of this second trip?' Scott enquired.

Tissa was cooperative, 'No problem, Scott, I will investigate it and get back to you. I will need to know the travel dates, and who will accompany him this time?'

The family decided this needed a family lunch involving Scott and Zelma. They were aware that Digby was becoming more stubborn and less spontaneous in cooperating with any idea mooted; and if left to keep going the way he was, he may become too entrenched in his ways and not treatable. Anything was worth a try and needed as many heads as possible to make the decision.

Scott was fully agreeable to the plan; Zelma was hesitant at first but decided to give any idea a try. She told John she wouldn't be able to travel with Digby, as he had not yet recognised her, and it would be too emotional an undertaking for her to handle. It therefore left John and Gladys to have to accompany him. John was receiving physiotherapy to aid in his recovery and was managing his wheelchair more confidently.

•••

Gladys organised a barbeque lunch on a Sunday, inviting Scott, Zelma and Jack as well. On Sunday, all the invitees arrived. This meal was going to be memorable and needed tact and diplomacy. After a hearty lunch, they all sat on the deck, wine glasses in hand. Digby became slowly more inebriated and jollier, alternating this with irritability. He needed to be introduced to the idea before he was totally out of it.

Scott opened the session, 'Digby, we are all happy to spend today with you, and wonder if you can remember any aspect of the past few months, especially your time in the jungle?'

Digby glanced all around him, not saying anything, trying as far as his mind allowed him to take in the seriousness of their faces, as they waited in anticipation to hear his every word.

'Jungle, which jungle?' he eagerly asked, sitting forward in his chair.

'I have some photographs taken whilst you were in the jungle, maybe they will help jog your memory,' Scott said, passing some pictures taken by Digby and others on the trips. 'They were taken in Sri Lanka, whilst you were trying to apprehend poachers who were killing elephants, leopard, and deer.'

Digby looked at them long and hard. 'I like them, they look familiar. So, what about them?'

'How would you like to return to those same jungles; this time most probably with your parents, but there will be no requirement to apprehend poachers?'

'Hmm, I'm not sure I would want to. This is where I live now. What's in it for me?' said an increasingly inquisitive Digby.

'For a start, your doctors say there is a strong possibility you will get your memory back and return to the man we all know and love and know is hiding inside you somewhere,' Scott went on. 'I have been in contact with Tissa, whom you may not recall, and you will stay at the same places you stayed in and visited before your injury. We all are sure you will enjoy it.'

'Hmm, going into a jungle is a sort of scary place for me – I'm not sure I want to do it. Why is everyone else deciding things for me?' Digby was now getting agitated, drank more beer and wanted to walk out from the lunch.

A hurried discussion took place. Zelma said she was not prepared to make the trip; Scott had work commitments, so it was left to John and Gladys to accompany him, much to John's annoyance, whilst Digby went for a walk around the garden.

Half an hour later a rather drunk Digby returned. 'Can someone convince me this is for my benefit? It seems a bizarre plan to me.'

Scott sternly asked, 'It's your doctor's treatment plan. Do you or do you not want to recover your memory?'

Digby was thoughtful. Then finally, he agreed. 'Alright I'll give it a try. I do want to recover my memory. When do we leave?'

In unison they all gave a mighty cheer. 'Hooray!' they shouted.

"We will organise the flights and the accommodation, coordinate with Tissa to leave as soon as possible, maybe in about ten days' time," said a very relieved Scott; John having to accept the plan, much against his will.

•••

Zelma had mixed feelings over all the negotiations. I do hope he doesn't deteriorate further and that he will improve and will eventually remember me. I must see where my life is heading, and don't want to rely too much on him; were her constant thoughts.

She needed to take a walk around the farm. Gladys joined her; knew Zelma felt alone now more than ever and tried to reassure her. A rather drunk and drowsy Digby caught up with them, but soon finding he was too intoxicated, returned to the house to fall asleep on the couch.

'I'm not sure what to make of all this. If things work out, I may have to make another trip to be with him, even though John and you are with him. I will have to prepare for any eventuality, I guess.' Zelma contemplated her possible next move with Gladys.

'My dear, let's take this slowly, one step at a time,' Gladys tried to comfort her.

Zelma felt a panic attack coming on, the rapid heart rate, nauseous feeling, perspiration, and stomach churnings. She had to sit down, take some deep breaths, close her eyes and imagine a tranquil scene of a palm-fringed beach. Gladys held her hand and sat beside her, Zelma really appreciating the kindly, mother in Gladys.

The afternoon ended with tea and cake, Zelma staying the night and Scott with Jack driving home just a few minutes' drive away.

The next morning an alert Digby, sat on the deck with Zelma, trying to connect with her. There was an awkward silence between them, Digby thoughtful and at a loss for words. Zelma decided she wouldn't rush him or put any pressure on him, they just talked about the weather and other mundane things, Zelma eventually deciding to return to Melbourne after breakfast.

FIFTEEN

RETURN TO THE SCENE OF THE CRIME

Three tickets were booked for leaving in ten days, and they were going into the dry season in Sri Lanka. Tissa was informed and he organised a four-wheel drive vehicle, and driver to collect them at the airport at midnight, John in his wheelchair, taking them to the same seaside hotel they had all used previously. On this trip they would move at a slower pace than before, allowing Digby time to get accustomed to one place, before moving onto the next wildlife park. John once again, organised a locum farmer to care for his animals and property, Digby's weekender now tenanted out. All the activity was confusing Digby, who didn't understand what was going on. He took himself off to find Jack with whom he seemed to have formed a kindred spirit. When he did locate him, at his home after work the two of them set off for the pub. This time John was able to locate him as he had his phone switched on. Being allowed just two drinks, put some restraints on his potential to become intoxicated. He continued to be disinhibited and loud mouthed, if he was not closely supervised, and Jack was doing this admirably well. His bags were packed by Gladys, just a rifle allowed this time, which John would take care of. Plenty of sunscreen and cool summer clothes being very necessary. The day of departure arrived, Digby better dressed this time, his hair cut short, clean shaven, smartly dressed clothes, all supervised by Gladys.

•••

Zelma and Scott were at the airport to wish them goodbye, and success in searching for restoration of Digby's memory, anything that would bring him back to his previous self. A miracle perhaps? They dared not dream; anything was possible. Digby was slowly beginning to understand that he was off on an overseas trip to the jungles and was seeing familiar faces in Scott and now Zelma. This was exciting for her.

'Have a successful trip, Digby, and hope to see you a different man when you return. I'm so looking forward to that day.' She gave him a formal kiss on his cheek, which he acknowledged with a smile.

'No worries, Zelma, I'm not sure what all this is about, but I sure hope to see you again, and certainly am looking forward to that day. I will try to make things happen.'

Scott gave Digby an affectionate embrace, telling him that he would keep in touch with all three of them when overseas.

After having their passports and tickets scanned, the three of them moved into the departure area, and through the large double doors into the customs area. As there was a three hour wait for departure, they decided to go for a slow meander along the duty-free shops and cafes at the terminal. Sitting down for a cup of coffee before their plane was due for departure Digby was becoming restless and distracted. He found it mundane sitting with his parents, so, looked around for a bit of adventure. He noticed some young females seated at the next table, giving them a few seductive glances. *Oh no,* thought John, *this is going to be embarrassing,* trying to distract his son with Gladys' assistance. Digby stood up appraising them, preparing to go over to their table, when, to everyone's huge relief, their male companions arrived taking them away.

John realised a trip on a crowded plane with an unwell son, may be more than he and Gladys could handle at their stage of life. The doctors had given them some anti-nausea tablets which also sedated and decided this would be a good time to give one to Digby, if he would take it. With much cajoling from his mother Digby eventually agreed to it, allowing them to sit back and relax before boarding. When called up to board the plane, they waited patiently before proceeding to their seats in the central aisle, and it wasn't long before the plane was full and ready for take-off.

The flight attendant assigned to their area was an attractive young woman dressed in a peacock blue sari, who Digby had his eye on, giving her admiring glances as she passed. A magazine produced by Gladys didn't distract him. However, some monks chanting at the back drew his attention, and he declared, 'I want to join those men at the rear,' and had to be forcefully restrained, before the tablets weaved their magic, and he was nodding off to sleep. Even a call for medical assistance didn't wake him from his slumber. The flight proceeded without any drama and they arrived at Colombo Airport at about midnight. The customs and visa process completed, they collected their baggage and headed out into the hot humid air of the tropics, a cool breeze blowing was a welcome tonic.

Arriving at the waiting area they met the same driver who was assigned to Digby on his previous trip; Dhanasiri, who greeted them with a warm smile, telling Digby, 'Hello, sir. Pleased to meet you again, and hope you all had a good trip,' holding both hands in namaste greeting.

Digby held out his hand for a handshake saying, 'Sorry, but I don't seem to remember who you are, but that seems to be the story of my life now.'

They alighted into the four-wheel drive vehicle and headed into the bright lights of Colombo. John and Gladys reminiscing on their previous trips, whilst trying to keep awake.

'Dhanasiri, there seems to be plenty of development here recently. The airport looks modern, and this road now a highway with no traffic lights to hold us up. I'm glad we can get to our hotel quickly. I guess Tissa has arranged all this, and we will stay in the same beautiful hotel we stayed in when on our previous visit?' Gladys asked.

'You are right, madam, the hotel will be about one hour's drive away, and at this time at night, there is no traffic on the roads.'

Arriving at the hotel, all the formalities completed, they sank into their comfortable beds for a good night's rest, extremely pleased with the adjoining rooms they were allocated facing the sea.

The next morning the tropical sun came streaming into their bedrooms, the cawing of crows a perfect alarm. John wandered into Digby's room to find him still asleep. After freshening up and an excellent cup of tea, they proceeded downstairs for the buffet breakfast. Being the same hotel Digby had stayed in on his last visit, there was a slight semblance of recognition. He noticed the wooden murals, the timber flooring, the saltwater swimming pool, the fish tank in the passageway, but not much else.

Tissa had wanted them to have a full day of rest before leaving for the countryside. John and Gladys were remembering the hotel, the sound of the tropics, the horns blaring and heavy traffic outside their window, and the children playing on the large green just outside their hotel. Breakfast was a delight to them especially Gladys remembering her childhood growing up on a tea estate and being served this type of food, looking out onto green pastures of well-maintained gardens, brought a tear to her eye. Eastern delights of hoppers, milk rice, curries, sambals, tropical fruit, as well as western food of all types. Pure Ceylon tea never tasted as good as in a Sri Lankan hotel.

After breakfast they ventured out of the hotel onto the roadside, being followed by men trying to tout a sale of either some handicrafts, or a ride in a three-wheeler to the city. 'Want a ride, madam? Very cheap! Only one hundred rupees to the Fort, I'll take you there.' Was voiced again and again, very annoying to some tourists, and interesting to others.

On the green lawn outside the street food sellers were in abundance. Fried green grams with a large fried prawn on top called vaddais, fried hot red chillies, casa casa seeds floating on a sweetened drink, all exotic and novel, but not for the uninitiated. Digby had flown many a kite on this green where the breezes blow in from the sea; had held the kite in the sky for hours. The blaring horns of the traffic as the vehicles passed by, the dust rising from the road, in the early morning it was not as bad as at midday when the sun was at its hottest. Digby wanted to join in with the local boys flying their kites, but his exuberance was a novelty, and they ran off.

To the western mind set it seemed like organised chaos; being pestered to be given unsolicited travel advice, being followed incessantly by layabouts trying to make a quick buck, the heat and humidity as the day wore on. The Trotts loved it, so different to their quiet home life on the farm. Digby tried out some Sinhala words, 'Ayubowan.' said with an Aussie accent brought shrieks of laughter from his newfound companions.

Returning to their hotel, they opted for a swim in the saltwater pool, as sea swimming at that location was prohibited as being too dangerous.

Lunch was a traditional rice and curry meal, which they hadn't tasted for years; or a lamprais meal where all the meats, vegetables and spices were melded together forming a delicious rice meal, sometimes wrapped in a banana leaf. Digby had a few glasses of wine which didn't suit his emotional stability, becoming over familiar with some of the other guests, much to their chagrin. John and Gladys had to exercise all their diplomacy and tact to keep him in rein, and they were glad when the evening and glorious sunset heralded night fall. There was a floor show after dinner of a king cobra brought in by a snake charmer of five cobras in wicker boxes, who swayed in sync to his flute keeping all the guests enthralled. This was one occasion Digby was mesmerised and quiet, as he tried to remember the snakes from his childhood in his parents' garden, and they had instilled in him a mortal fear of all snakes, especially cobras. 'I can picture a large king cobra at the bottom of grandpa's garden, and it is eating baby birds in their nest. Grandpa had to shoot that nasty snake,' John amazed at his memory in remembering that incident.

•••

Gladys was in a nostalgic mood, when she reminded John, 'I remember growing up on Dad and Mum's beautiful estate surrounded by hundreds of acres of tea bushes, of going into the tea factory and watching how tea leaves were picked and dried and eventually packeted for sale. Bad memories of going to boarding school, of crying my eyes out at night as I missed home.'

'You poor thing. But the good times came when I met you, and the fun times we had going out together when I worked in the hill country, of our wedding and raising Digby in his primary school years. Yes, they were definitely good times.'

In the cool of the evening the air was soft and limpid as they sat around the pool soaking in the sea breezes. The sea just outside the low wall looked splendid as the small waves broke on the shore. It was such nostalgia, but they both had to remind themselves of the serious and possibly dangerous mission they were now embroiled in.

They both got out of their daydream and had to now focus on their son's new chapter of his life.

•••

The next day after breakfast, Dhanasiri arrived to take them on their first lap of Digby's return journey. They would travel via Ratnapura to reach Buttala at night fall, a few hundred kilometres away. The city of gems beckoned Gladys who was captivated by precious stones, and she had to stop at Ratnapura and check out the beautiful sapphires, boring Digby who was getting restless to keep going.

'Why do you need to look at these pieces of jewellery?' he impatiently asked. 'They look like nothing more than glass!' He paced up and down along the road whilst whistling as he walked.

Gladys tried to ignore him as she gazed into the cabinets storing the gems; *maybe I'll get a necklace for Zelma* she quietly contemplated as she made her purchase, hoping it was not an imitation and the real thing.

Onward through countless traffic jams, blaring horns and negotiating cattle, stray dogs, buses, trishaws, and lorries on the road, they kept on with their journey. At about lunch time they stopped for a typical rice and curry lunch at the Rest House at Haputale overlooking tea bushes in the hill country. This reminded Gladys of her childhood in a similar locale, and tears welled up in her eyes looking at the beautiful scenery. The air fresh and crisp, so unlike the heat of the low country, she felt she could sit there forever.

After lunch they were held up in their journey by a religious festival procession of dancers, elephants, and young girls dressed in white, waving flags.

'Dhanasiri, why is this procession on today?' John asked.

'It is full moon night tonight, and Buddhists celebrate full moon with a public holiday every month, sir.'

Digby not appreciating the culture, was giggling quietly, showing callous unconcern for the feelings of others. Nobody else thought it was funny. It made Dhanasiri wonder *What has happened to the dear friend Mr Digby I knew and drove around?*

It was getting darker after sunset, as they approached Buttala. With not many other vehicles on the unlit road the car head lights lit up a pair of eyes seated on the road, which bounded away into the undergrowth by the side of the road. Dhanasiri said, 'I just saw a leopard or jungle cat run off the road.'

'Where, where?' they all said in unison, but it was too late to spot any wildlife.

Travelling on the lonely country road, with no street lighting was a nerve-wracking journey. After another few kilometres, the car screeched to a halt, as a small herd of four elephants were crossing the road just outside the village of Wellawaya before their destination of Buttala. John held his chest, saying.

'My goodness, this fright isn't good for my heart!'

Gladys screamed out in fear, but Digby peering into the darkness, looked on helplessly. He was taking in the scene quietly. The elephants appeared to come towards their vehicle forcing Dhanasiri to reverse in a hurry and hold out the palm of his hand to them shouting 'Dhana. Dhana' meaning 'Stop. Stop' which seemed to work, much to everybody's relief, as the enormous beasts turned and walked into the jungle.

It seemed like adequate excitement for one day, and it was with a sigh of relief that they reached their bungalow in Buttala, just outside town, to be greeted by the same cook cum house boy Digby had met on his previous visit, but who he didn't remember on this occasion. After a hearty rice and curry meal they sat on the verandah under oil lamps listening to the sounds of the jungle, and the house geckos on the walls. Fireflies were buzzing around the trees, and the shrill sound of cicadas broke the silence. It had the sound of a sort of fury. Then suddenly it was silenced by the loud singing of a bird. At night the frogs croak, croak, croak. After a while, the evening heat became hot and humid but with a cool breeze blowing through the house, they all retired under mosquito nets for a good night's sleep.

• • •

The morning sun greeted them with rays of gold streaming into the house. Two black birds darted around on the lawn outside, and the shrill call of a pea fowl echoed throughout the jungle. Around the house there was an abundance of fresh green vegetation; the bougainvillea in shades of pink and purple fell in cascades looking wonderfully radiant, whilst the colourful parrots darted around the red-wattled lapwing, making its 'did you do it' sound magical to the ears.

The cook had made for them a typical breakfast of milk rice, hot coconut sambal and fish curry; such a tasty treat, and they savoured the flavours with delight. They then joined Dhanasiri in his four-wheel drive vehicle to set off for a trip into the Yala National Park. They had brought typical jungle safari gear of khaki shorts and tops.

Digby exclaimed, 'I'm so excited to be going into the jungle, I can hear shrill bird calls, elephants trumpeting, the timid cries of a deer, and the loud call of the peacock. Let's make this happen. I can't wait.'

'Yes Digby, this is your adventure… it's all up to you.' John looked hard at his son.

He was surprised to see the reaction of Digby to the return of his adventures. Something he hadn't expected of him, but extremely pleased for him.

It was a good half hour's drive to the Barrier Gate, along a long, sandy, dusty road. They set off before the heat of the midday sun would consume their energy and arrived at the barrier gate to collect the necessary tracker cum guide. It was envisioned that Digby would try and recall as much as he could of his previous trip.

On entering the park, they noticed a dead elephant lying near the entrance, the tracker saying,

'The wildlife officers said that most probably the elephant has been poisoned but they don't know by whom. It has been dead for a few days now. We are not allowed to get down from the vehicle and look at the dead animal.'

Digby was eager to have a closer look and was disappointed at not being allowed to do so. He appeared to be hatching a plan.

'Sir, if you want to get down and walk, the sand dunes by the beach are the place where it can be done,' the tracker added.

They drove on to locate the watch huts, and passed a herd of deer, where again Digby wanted to get out and touch the animals and couldn't understand why he wasn't able to. Eventually, they stopped the vehicle by the sea at the beach and they all alighted and walked along the dunes. Whilst the others were looking out to sea, Digby decided to go off on his own and soon disappeared from the others. When they turned around, they found him gone.

As shouting was disallowed in the park, they couldn't scream out his name, and started to panic. The tracker asked the others to get back into the vehicle and went out on foot searching for Digby, who had wandered further into the jungle, and had come upon fresh paw marks of a leopard. He knew, even in his confused state, that this was dangerous. Both the tracker and Digby heard the sawing of a leopard, and Digby decided to climb a low tree to get a vantage view of the jungle. The tracker was beginning to despair of finding him, especially as he wasn't supposed to walk too far from the vehicle. He returned to the others not having located Digby. They all began to panic; this time Dhanasiri and the tracker set out to locate him, as the sawing became louder, then stopped. The two of them held their chests and looked around. A branch fell from a tree, and they looked up- to see Digby seated on a large branch. Feeling extreme relief, they motioned for him to descend, but he refused. Dhanasiri pleaded softly, 'Please sir, there is a leopard around here, can you quietly come down.'

'No, I like it here. I can see everything around me.'

The sawing started again, then a growl. The tracker shouted out and screamed. He then fired a shot into the air. Digby, realising the situation, slowly descended from his lofty perch. Together they ran back towards their vehicle. Panting they reached it and scrambled inside, and Dhanasiri starting the engine immediately.

John, livid with his son, screamed at him, 'What on earth are you thinking, wandering off into thick jungle with dangerous animals? This could have been a disaster. You will stay close to us at all times, and that is an order. You could have been killed, together with the other two.'

'Well, I know now. I'll try and be careful,' he said, sounding sheepish.

•••

The party drove around Block one of the Yala Park and located the wattle and daub watch huts, with thatched roofs made from the branches of the coconut palm. The tracker looked up into the roof of one hut and noticed a very long python sleeping in the eaves. This was scary. They surveyed another watch hut further away and scrutinised it carefully, deciding no snakes had taken refuge in it, as well as another one which seemed safe. They marked the safe huts to be used for their night stay.

Digby remarked, 'I seem to remember something of these huts that we stayed in before, but it is very foggy. I wish I could remember more.'

John wasn't too sure that staying in the isolated huts in the jungle with no lights other than powerful torches, and perhaps an oil lamp they brought in, would be a good idea with a footloose and amnesic son to keep an eye on. But there didn't seem to be an alternative, so he reckoned.

Digby, however, was getting excited at the sense of adventure that could lie ahead if they decided to stay a night or two or maybe three. As the Melbourne doctors had recommended that going through as much as he was put through as on his first visit would stir his memory, there was much to think about and decide on.

'Dhanasiri, you were with us on my earlier visit, can you please refresh my memory. I seem to recall a few things here and there, like the watch huts we just drove past.'

'Yes sir, there were several of us; Palitha, the driver, Sunil and Bandara and later Anura and Gamini. I will take you all to look inside the watch huts.'

Driving back to the huts Digby walked inside and had a look around, a thoughtful look came over his face. 'Did you say we stayed in these huts?' he asked Dhanasiri. 'I am trying to remember what it was like. Keep talking, I want to picture our last trip. Maybe it will come to me slowly, I'm certainly hoping…'

John had a look at the huts and wasn't impressed. They were too basic, with only camp beds, mosquito netting and a kerosene cooker. They had to bring in all provisions, water and mosquito coils, not to mention roll-on mosquito prevention. Fortunately, there were doors to these huts, so necessary to keep out wandering and dangerous wildlife.

Dhanasiri remembered the elephant chase telling Digby, 'Sir, you may remember the elephant that charged us when Palitha was driving. We were all terrified.'

A thoughtful Digby looked around, 'Perhaps, if you can remember where that took place you could take us there.'

'Not sure I can remember that spot, sir, it was at the spot where the road branches in two directions, and there are so many places like that here.'

●●●

As the afternoon sun was now directly overhead and the day was getting hotter, they headed back to their base. After a tasty rice and curry meal John and Gladys, feeling the heat, decided to have an afternoon nap; but Digby wandering off was a worry, so

Dhanasiri said he would keep an eye on him. They tried to sleep, but in the intense heat they came out into the veranda, drowsy, the air hot and stifling. Limited electricity meant small fans were circulating hot air which were of little use. Trying to go back to sleep they threw themselves back onto their beds under the mosquito netting where the air seemed to stand still. Trying to read, or think was useless. The only way to cool themselves was to take a shower, in cold water, which offered some relief. A few cold beers were a bonus.

The screeching of a flight of birds was a welcome distraction, whilst they prepared for the afternoon trip back into the wildlife park to further check out blocks one and two.

John spoke to Dhanasiri, 'I think it is too risky sleeping in the watch huts with Digby trying to wander off. We must return here for the night. We will drive around and get our bearings, of Blocks one and two and return here for the night.'

The afternoon trip did not yield much more than what they saw on the morning round; a few crocodiles, plenty of deer and a herd of elephants. As luck would have it there was a leopard sitting up in the branch of a tree having a sleep, oblivious to watching human eyes. A few other tourist vehicles passed them excited to see the leopard asleep on its perch. Digby sat quietly throughout the trip, seeming to take in all that was going on, and not conversing very much. At dusk they decided to head back to the Buttala bungalow to watch the sun set over the water tank, magnificently, yellow, then red and purple, and in the distance, coconut trees on the bank reflected in the water, as well as the sun's ray of gold reflecting on the water, a delightful scene.

The bungalow had an open veranda where beds were laid out with mosquito nets over them. There was a cool breeze blowing through the house which was refreshing. The sound of millions of cicadas broke the silence, the little lizards, or *chik-chaks* on the walls were loud and intense. They were relaxing after a hearty dinner, and then they settled down for the night.

•••

At about midnight there was a loud trumpeting of elephants just outside their bungalow; flashing torches, Dhanasiri and the cook saw a herd of about six elephants, perhaps five hundred metres away. The leader, an enormous tusker had his trunk raised and was waving it from side to side attempting to sniff the air for the scent of humans, is what it seemed to be.

Panic gripped all the party waking them from their sleep. The cook said the elephants were looking for food where they knew there were humans. With no tracker to control the elephants all the occupants in the house were in real danger. Hurriedly they packed into their four-wheel drive, in their night clothes, and Dhanasiri drove as fast as he could onto the main road, as far away from the enormous beasts as possible. Everyone was in a state of indescribable fright. It was a wonder he could even drive, his hands were shaking, his heart pounding, and perspiration pouring down his neck.

Gladys kept repeating, 'My God. My God,' and she held tightly onto John.

Digby was shouting, 'Where the fricking hell are we going? Those animals can kill us.'

After driving down the dark, deserted road for about twenty minutes, they stopped and took stock of the situation. The cook saying, "never before have I seen this happen."

The elephants were becoming more audacious and bolder. The Trotts sat in their vehicle for an hour, and then drove back to survey the damage, and there was plenty. In attempting to plunder food from the kitchen the pachyderms had pulled down the veranda, broken the glass windows and devoured all the fruit and vegetable they could get their trunks onto in the process. The house was a mess, debris scattered everywhere, and the invaders nowhere to be seen. Were they close to the house? Not being certain, John decided to move to the local Rest House for the remainder of the night. Alternate accommodation had to be found, Tissa again to the rescue. He organised a house with adequate space in Buttala town, which was ideal.

The shock to all of them seemed to influence Digby especially, and he remarked, 'I feel a fuzzy sensation in my head and am sort of remembering a few details of staying where we did: I can sort of recognise Dhanasiri now.'

John and Gladys were over the moon, 'I guess the doctors back in Australia were correct, but I doubt Gladys and I can take any more shocks to our hearts – we are getting too old for this type of adventure,' John exclaimed, holding his chest.

They had to remain where they were for another day and night to facilitate entry into the Yala Park. A bungalow inside the park was available, and Tissa suggested they move in there, but they were too terrified to stay inside the park at the mercy of all that wildlife. Digby, deep in thought, appeared to be hatching something.

SIXTEEN

DIGBY GOES MIISSING

The morning sun came streaming into their bedrooms; the entire party decided to sleep in after all the terror and excitement they had been through. Going into Digby's room they found his bed empty and the sheets barely disturbed. Panic went through all their minds; they started calling out to him, but there was no response. They didn't know where to start looking. John and Gladys wanted to get into their vehicle and go searching for him.

Dhanasiri said, 'There is only one road that leads into this town, and Digby must walk on it to get anywhere. He must have left at night, and he could have gone into the jungle. We can call out to him as we go along.'

They drove along the lonely country road, stopping frequently and with a loudspeaker called out, 'Digby! Digby, where are you?' but only silence greeted them.

Birds called out as if in reply, yet only the echoes of their voices reverberated back to them.

After driving up and down that road for one hour, finding him on their own seemed futile. They had to inform the Tourist Police. The police set about sending out a search party to scour the area which had jungle on both sides of the road; with loudspeakers blaring, the police drove around at slow speed.

•••

Digby had gone into a section of the jungle and came upon a small chena clearing where villagers were growing corn and vegetables around their three mud huts. The villagers were surprised to see a white man arrive at their little compound, especially as he spoke limited Sinhala and they spoke no English. To their simple way of life, he appeared confused and incoherent, as if drunk. Asking him his name – *numma* – he couldn't remember anything to answer them. They took him in to one of the huts and gave him water, as he indicated in sign language that he was thirsty. He was tired from walking on the hot sandy undergrowth, breaking branches as he walked along. One of the men decided to get out onto the main road to locate any passing traffic, but only a three-wheeler went past him in a hurry. The man decided to keep walking until he came to the Police Station, the police sending out a search party into the jungle chena to find him.

John and Gladys sat in the police jeep whilst two policemen walked in to the jungle, but when they arrived at the huts Digby had disappeared again. It was getting darker, and light was fading, and they were beginning to despair that he would be located before nightfall. Loudspeakers were not helping. His footprints were followed up to a point but disappeared soon after that. He wasn't wearing warm clothing and had no food or water on him. John, Gladys and Dhanasiri were beside themselves with worry.

As dusk fell, and with no sign of Digby they had no option but to call off the search until daybreak.

With heavy hearts and worried minds, they returned to their bungalow, but nobody could fall asleep, they just kept a vigil until daybreak.

Digby had been staggering around the undergrowth until he collapsed on the ground underneath a large tree and fell asleep, with mosquitoes and insects swirling around him. As the darkness of night enveloped him, jackals were wailing around him, and one or two came by to sniff at him. He was too asleep to notice them, then an elephant's trumpeting in the distance, disturbed the night. He woke with a start, not knowing where he was, with only fireflies to light the way he tried to stand up but was too sleepy to take more than a few steps, he fell back to sleep again. At daybreak he staggered around and sat down huddled up for warmth hoping a search party would locate him.

Renewing the search in the morning, and armed with sniffer dogs, and loudspeakers the police were out looking for him again. This time it didn't take long for a dog to trace the scent of his clothes to where he was staggering around, covered in insect bites, and he sat down again, as the police located him. He needed to go into hospital for fluid resuscitation and a check-up. After a short stay in hospital, he was discharged, tired but well. John and Gladys now despairing of the responsibility of caring for their son.

'What the hell were you thinking disappearing into the jungle? There are wild and dangerous animals out there. You could have been killed.' John was livid with him once again for the irresponsible behaviour, but he was unsure if he was getting through to him.

Digby looked remorseful for once but couldn't find words to placate his irate father. 'Sorry, Dad,' was all he could offer.

•••

John and Gladys decided not to proceed with any more trips into the Yala Game Park, as that park seemed to stir up a kind of confusion in their son, and they reckoned driving around the park with no definite plan wasn't something they felt was warranted. A couple of days' rest in their comfortable home seemed in the best interests of everyone.

The next morning, they woke to the sounds of the jungle, a cup of tea on the veranda and a Lankan breakfast of string hoppers, egg curry, and coconut sambal. A rural landscape and twittering birds outside their bungalow were calming and delightful. The pea fowl's cry was always the most musical to their ears. Gladys remembered some of her Sinhala from her many years in the country of her birth and enjoyed communicating with the cook and Dhanasiri whenever she had the opportunity.

•••

Two days later they set off after breakfast to the next stop at the Gal Oya Wildlife Park. The road was dusty and unmade and took them firstly to Monaragala, a small hamlet en route, a short distance from where they left at Buttala. The next stop for a cuppa was Pallewela for a leg stretch and a short break. The paddy fields as they passed were in full harvest, delighting Gladys, the work being done manually, no machinery in those hamlets. Onwards to the Inginiyagala Circuit Bungalow just outside the Gal Oya Park, where both Digby and Dhanasiri had stayed on his previous visit. A beautiful, spacious house where Podi Singho the in-house cook greeted Digby,

'Hello, sir, it is so nice to see you again. I hope you had a nice trip coming here, no?'

'Do I know you? I can't recall seeing you before today.'

Podi Singho seemed taken aback, 'Why not, sir, you said how much you liked the hoppers I made for you. I'll make them again. Maybe when you taste them you will remember me?'

'That will be excellent. Then maybe my parents too can sample your delicious cooking.'

They settled into their accommodation, hoping for an evening trip into the park, but the weather gods had different ideas – it was going to be a rainy day. There was a moaning of thunder in the distance, and one by one fell the first drops of rain; it was like the tears of God. Was this a good omen? Maybe not, that's what Gladys reckoned.

Tissa wanted Palitha, Digby's previous driver, to take them into the Gal Oya Park, hoping it might jog his memory, seeing his former driver at the wheel. He dispatched Palitha with Sunil and Bandara from the previous trip to accompany the Trott family as he determined Dhanasiri had enough of an exciting time and needed a break from driving.

Palitha greeted Digby with hands held in namaste saying, 'Ayubowan, sir, nice to see you again.'

Digby looked hard at Palitha. 'I've seen you somewhere in the past and I'm trying to remember where in the past and wish I can remember.'

'Why not, sir? I drove you around on your last trip to all the Game Parks,' Palitha replied to a thoughtful Digby.

'Hmm.'

•••

Tissa informed John that the Gal Oya Park had no tourists, and the watch huts were in a state of disrepair needing necessities to be taken into the huts from the town of Ampara. A drive to Ampara at midday in intense eastern Sri Lankan heat, not to be enjoyed, making it a quick trip. Back at their circuit bungalow, they tried to settle into their land locked destination, a cool breeze blowing in to rid the house of hot air. A cold shower helped reduce the extreme perspiration, aided by fans. No air conditioning luxury here.

At five pm Palitha drove the family with Sunil and Bandara into the Park after collecting the compulsory tracker. Digby was overjoyed to be in dense jungle saying, 'Oh, to be back in this tropical wonderland again. The smell of green vegetation, the sight of shy animals scurrying away, always makes me smile.'

Driving past a herd of about twenty elephants – seeking solace from the heat – under a tree, brought excitement to the party.

The tracker saying, 'Look, there are two babies near their mothers, they look about two months old. We must be quiet so as not to disturb them. The best way to see them is to use a boat on the Samudra or large tank, and we can observe them as we did on the previous trip, if you can remember that sir?' to Digby, who didn't seem to recall the boat ride. The boat ride was exciting to John who needed help getting into the boat, and Gladys, peering into the distance trying to locate elephants and buffalo, but they were not rewarded with any sightings.

After the boat trip, they toured the park having a look at the watch huts. John had a look inside and was ambivalent as to whether it was safe to take Digby inside in his present state, but as his memory was now showing signs of recall, decided they had to follow the doctor's instructions.

They returned to their base, had lunch and at about five pm, and returned to the watch huts to settle in for the night. The sky seen through the tall trees surrounding the hut was slate grey, and so drab and melancholy was its colour that it seemed a work of man. It was the colour of infinite sorrow. Rain was on the horizon. They had the watch huts to themselves, seven of them requiring two huts with camp beds and mosquito netting.

Digby was playing at somnolence and chose to hit the hay about nine pm, but he was hatching a plan to try and slip out to investigate, with his small pocket torch lighting the way, being a moonless night. Very soon the rest of the party were deep in slumber and having no doors to exit he slipped out into the darkness following a route he thought led him to the water's edge a few hundred yards from the watch huts. He did recall the elephants somewhere around there.

After a few minutes he heard voices and saw in the light of the flickering fireflies that poachers were creeping up to the herd, and one man was trying to steal a baby from the herd, as the baby was on the outer with its mother. The poacher did grab the baby, which let out a squeal, and out came the mother thundering after the man who was running as fast as he could, but he stood no chance. As silently as it came the elephant knocked the man down with its trunk and stood on his head with its forefoot, the man screaming for his life, whilst the other poachers scattered very swiftly. Digby witnessing this spectacle with his penlight torch and in a state of utter fight tried to run behind a bush but fell over, then lay very still. The elephant, trumpeting loudly, retreated into the jungle.

The entire party in the watch huts heard the commotion and checked Digby's bed where he had supposedly fallen asleep that night, to find him missing. Fearing the worst, and with 4D cell torches, with the tracker leading the way, set out to find him in the darkness of the eerie night. The wind being in their favour, they quietly wound their way towards the water's edge. Digby, trembling with fear, saw the torch lights from a distance and proceeded very cautiously in that direction. Catching up with his rescuers they all wound their arms around him. He was trembling and shaking and had to hold onto them for a few minutes.

'I just witnessed an attack by an elephant on a man, and he is lying dead somewhere in the jungle. That was the most horrible thing I have ever seen,' Digby muttered in a shaky, soft voice, his heart beating out of his chest. 'I think he was trying to steal a baby elephant.'

They had to all sit down and take it in quietly. Digby was beginning to mutter incoherently and was trembling, feeling hot to the touch. He may have had a fever, is what his mother reckoned. After 30 minutes he was half carried by Sunil and Bandara back to the watch huts. The sagacious tracker advised against trying to locate the dead man, saying it could be done in the morning. He decided to place his bed between his parents, still shaking from the ordeal.

The next morning four of the party set out at dawn retreating their steps from the previous night to locate the dead man, but despite scouring the thick undergrowth, there was no sign of him. They did notice some blood on the ground where he was killed.

The tracker remarked, 'I'd say the other poachers must have returned and taken his body away,' to which they all agreed, being relieved not having to witness the gruesome sight of human remains. Just remembering the ordeal was nauseating enough.

The team then returned to their base at the circuit bungalow. Digby plumbed the depths of his memory to recall the Gal Oya Park and the present bungalow where he had stayed during his past trip. He could vaguely remember Podi Singho, who was overjoyed.

'Now that I've eaten your delicious hoppers, I can sort of remember being here, but it is still indistinct,' Digby said to the cook, who was happy to help jog Digby's returning memory.

They remained at Gal Oya doing drives into the park in the morning and afternoon for the next twenty-four hours, before planning their next move to the much larger Wilpattu National Park. Foot safaris being permitted, they did get out and walk about the park, bearing in mind, as the tracker reminded them, that every stick could be a snake, and to tread with caution. True enough, whilst walking amongst dry leaves on the road a snake slid out from the undergrowth, which turned out to be a king cobra. Sensing movement, it lifted its head to strike. The tracker noticed this and swung into action, pushing Digby and Gladys out of its path. Deciding there was too much at stake whilst on a walking tour, they jumped into the vehicle for a safer trip.

'That was a near miss,' said Gladys, shaking with fright. 'I have a morbid fear of snakes, especially cobras.'

Being the end of the dry season most of the water holes had little water, with plenty of crocodiles basking in the sun. Elephants were plentiful, whereas other larger wildlife in scarcity. After long drives they decided that the park had yielded as much as they could absorb. It was now time to take a break before their next stop.

SEVENTEEN

BACK TO WILPATTU

The final scheduled stop was to the Wilpattu Game Park. Digby's memory seemed to have been jolted several times, and he was quietly remembering a few incidents; was not as obnoxious and flippant, altogether becoming a more pleasant man, much to the delight of his parents, as well as all the others in the team.

They left the next morning, waking early to journey through Bibile, and then onto Kandy for lunch. Getting to Puttalam was a long and tiring trip, requiring a night stop over at Kurunegala for an early sleep at the local Rest House. Being a winding road Gladys suffered motion sickness, which distressed her, as up to now she had travelled well. A trip to the ancient historic Temple of the Tooth in Kandy was planned, if that could be scheduled, and Digby was rational and manageable. The others in the team were eager to visit the temple, sacred to Buddhists, which was easily accommodated.

'Look, look at the monkeys in play,' Gladys eagerly announced, as they ran off with bananas thrown at them, and scrambled up tree trunks. Several hundred grey monkeys were scrambling over ruins whilst playing with each other, loving humans watching them.

'I remember the ruins which are memorable from my childhood days,' she enthused.

Digby was trying to recall seeing them in his childhood, especially during his visits to the Colombo Zoo, or on other holiday trips.

'I seem to remember seeing these monkeys stealing food left around, and climbing tall coconut trees,' he muttered to his father.

'That's a good sign, we must keep working on jolting your memory,' John turned to his son, in delight.

•••

It was late afternoon when they checked into the Rest House, for a well-earned rest in the large town of Kurunegala. Being a rain-soaked day and the necessity of driving through numerous traffic jams, with buses and three wheelers holding up traffic, it was slow travel. No traffic rules, just horn blaring, and negotiating space to put your vehicle through. The hoots of the motor-horns, and the roar of the exhausts choking an already smog-filled environment with more fumes and dust. No traffic lights, just a lone traffic policeman trying to direct hundreds of vehicles and failing miserably. It was an oasis, in the chaos of the traffic, to sit back and relax in large lounge chairs in the garden of the rest house. An early dinner and early bed were on the agenda for all of them.

The next day they left for the hour-and-a-half trip to Puttalam, and into the park bungalow inside the Wilpattu Game Park, after collecting the tracker at the barrier gate. The Mardanmaduwa Bungalow, organised by Tissa, had a magnificent view of the large water tank a few hundred yards away where animals especially elephants, deer and the occasional leopard came to drink. No watch huts were planned in this park as they were too isolated and dangerous for Digby, the entire team having concurred with this decision. It didn't take long to settle into this comfortable house, as there was plenty of space for everyone. Digby was to share with his parents on this occasion. Sunil and Bandara had another room, and the two drivers and tracker, the third room. Tissa had hoped to join them here, but work commitments had kept him busy. A 'Cook's Tour' was planned for early the next morning after they collected food supplies from the nearest town.

John declared, 'I would love to drive around and get a feel for the landscape here.' Being in the northwest part of the island, and in the dry zone of the country, the ground was parched. Trees which were evergreen showed shades of green, others had wilted dry leaves, and tall coconut trees were plentiful. The ground was strewn with dry leaves and dry twigs. The main feature of Wilpattu was the beautiful freshwater lakes each called a *villu* in Tamil, another part of the landscape being the terrain, gently undulating leading down to the sand- rimmed water with tall dense forest surrounding the water and the green pastures.

Gladys remarked, 'How peaceful this park is, not too many humans, just water, vegetation and animals. Beautiful lotus is in abundance in the water.'

Taking a drive around the park, they encountered large herds of elephants, a leopard with her two cubs seated under a tree, and hundreds of deer, and wild boar who may frequently get into a fight to the death with a leopard.

Digby was observing all the animals quietly, not saying much. When quiet, he was a worry to all the others as he often seemed to be hatching a plan.

Gladys was keen to see even one sloth bear, and her wish was granted, as a furtive, shy bear slunk away from their vehicle as it approached. The famous white deer of Wilpattu were not to be seen on their outing. After their drive they all settled in for a quiet – or so they hoped – evening in their bungalow.

The cool of the evening with the air soft and limpid, came with an extreme sense of wellbeing, giving Digby a sort of sense of freedom. The half-moon was just beginning to show itself where the jungle spread densely. Many a violent animal could have been shrouded in the thick foliage, perhaps waiting for an unexpected event. The frogs croaked and the cicadas with their awful noise had a sort of fury, seeming like they would never shut up. Fireflies gave the shrubs the look of a Christmas tree, all lit up and sparkling softly – the radiance of a soul at peace – which belied the dangers within the jungle.

With the clouds above looking tortured, and in the faint glimpse of a setting sun, they all settled down to dinner and quiet relaxation before hitting the hay in the open veranda under mosquito nets, to the sounds of the jungle at night. The occasional sawing of a leopard, the frightened bark of a deer, the bark of a jackal, all unnerving when heard in the darkness of night.

The next morning, they woke to the crowing of a jungle fowl strident and loud, to sit out in the garden and watch a pale blue sky with the languor of oncoming great heat. In the early morning, the colours of the jungle were brilliant yet tender, and as the day wore on, they were tired with the various tones of heat.

Showers were cold, the water being pumped up from a deep well, invigorating, yet not unpleasant. A breakfast of Sri Lankan delicacies awaited them, food to stir nostalgic memories of times past such as hoppers, string hoppers and milk rice with sambals and curries washed down with fresh tea. They all then set out on a tour of the park downwards to the water's edge of the giant tanks, reviving Digby's memory of his previous trip.

Palitha at the wheel, they then drove past the watch huts where Digby last stayed before his attack.

'Mind if I stop for a while?' he tentatively enquired.

'Of course, sir, we can certainly stop for a while.'

The tracker and Digby got out to have a look declaring them basic and in need of work.

'Glad we're not staying here. They look like they are un-inhabitable,' the tracker remarked.

Digby was quiet, not wishing to make any comment.

Getting back to their vehicle, a full-grown cobra slithered out of the undergrowth between Digby, the tracker and their vehicle; it then raised its hood into the striking position. Digby stepped back in horror, the tracker saying, 'Stand still, don't move.'

John remembered that it follows the vibration of the ground as it can't see that well and it also can't hear, and it uses its tongue to search the surroundings. After a few hearts stopping minutes the king cobra slithered away into the undergrowth, much to the relief of everybody around it.

Whilst driving around, they noticed that there were several herds of elephants, especially around the many water holes and water tanks, some herds as many as fifty to sixty in numbers. There were a few baby elephants in the herd, which fascinated Gladys and Digby. As the afternoon heat began to wear them down, John and Gladys decided to return to the cool of the bungalow, the others concurring.

•••

Walking around the bungalow being allowed, Digby wandered

off, walking down to the water's edge, where the water in the centre was clear, but marsh reeds and mud with water lilies in it lay towards the boundary. The elephant herd was only a few hundred metres away in the jungle, although he was unaware of their location, the wind in his favour. A baby elephant by the water's edge, had somehow managed to become separated from its mother, and squealed in fright, possibly from loneliness. Digby seemed quite concerned and excited for this baby animal, and in trying to reach out for it slipped into the muddy waters and appeared to sink further into the mud, with no one from his party around. He had armed himself with his rifle when he left the bungalow and tried not to let it be submerged. He found his feet stuck in the mud and used as much energy as he could to extricate them with some success.

On the horizon a dark wall of six-ton bodies was headed towards the water and reached the deep water, starting to wallow in the mud, making an awful lot of noise.

Fifty metres away a young bull appeared, its trunk lifted in the air with only its tip bent, its ears stiff and standing at right-angles to its head. Its small terrifying cyes wide open showing only the whites fixed and flashing, it came crashing towards Digby. Instinctively, he moved to his left and into more mud and reeds whilst the elephant crashed into the water. In Digby's confused mind he was unaware of the real danger he was in.

The crashing and splashing of the herd had ceased with sudden silence, which meant that many of the herd had reached a deep part of the tank and were wallowing in the muddy water.

Digby tried to move and found he was stuck further in the mud. He fired a shot into the air and screamed as loudly as he could. At these sounds, about thirty elephant trunks went straight up into the air. The bull turned, his oral cavity being fully exposed in full view of the bank where a terrified tracker was standing, gun in hand, and he fired straight into the elephant's mouth. He collapsed, dying, and landed in a heap into the water at Digby's feet.

With the sound of the shots the herd disintegrated into groups of about ten each and started running madly out of the water in different directions, back up the hill from where they came.

Digby realised he had to get away as quickly as he could, and scrambled to free himself out of the mud, the tracker attempting to come near him and assist him. They suddenly heard the cries of the baby elephant, the calls coming at regular intervals which sounded like it was crying for its mother, who may have fled with the herd. The calf pushed towards Digby, to be near another living creature, the tracker advising Digby to get away quickly, as the mother would come looking for her calf. However, the calf clung to Digby's heels and was attempting to follow him. The mother elephant suddenly came out of nowhere and charged straight at Digby who had lost his rifle and couldn't fire, but the tracker fired again, whilst Digby fell back into the muddy water and reeds. The elephant had not collapsed so the tracker fired another shot straight at the heart, with blood gushing everywhere she was not dead yet. She lifted her trunk trying to get the scent of man, then wound her trunk around her baby, swung it above the water and hurled the baby down at her feet. Collapsing, with her last breath she smothered her own child to death.

Digby, witnessing this horrible spectacle, collapsed into the water semiconscious; his life had clearly hung on a thread, and the situation had certainly gone down to the wire; were his thoughts as he drifted into a sleepy haze. He had hurt his left ankle and couldn't walk. The tracker helped him stagger out of the water, and with the aid of Dhanasiri, into a vehicle nearby.

All the while, John, Gladys and the others had been witnessing the horror aghast, their hearts beating out of their chests, and all blood drained from their faces. A wet and limp Digby was taken to the bungalow, and after a change of clothes lay down to sleep exhausted and in a state of stupor.

The elephants later returned to view the dead members of their herd; a cow, a young male and a calf, touching them with their trunks and talking softly amongst themselves. They had come to mourn their dead.

That afternoon, John called a meeting of the entire team to get their views.

'I feel we are all in danger, as I understand that elephants never forget, and the herd may return to seek revenge. I would like to propose to Tissa that we move out of this bungalow and we need to admit Digby into hospital.'

The tracker added, 'Sir, in the past elephants have sometimes surrounded this bungalow, as it is so close to the water where they gather. They may surround this place today when they come back to see their dead.' So, it was decided they had to move immediately to another residence.

Digby was muttering, 'I must get away, I must run away,' and he was hot to the touch.

A phone call to Tissa was made and he hurriedly organised alternate accommodation in the town of Puttalam. Digby was admitted to hospital, running a fever and talking incoherently. He needed hospital observation. John and Gladys were concerned he may have suffered permanent brain damage and maintained a vigil by his bedside all night.

The next morning, he was drowsy and still muttering under his breath. He needed fluids by drip and further observation, whilst his exhausted and worried parents returned to get some rest themselves. The entire team visited Digby, alone or in pairs, whilst he was recovering slowly in hospital. After three days he was more alert and looked around him furtively, eating well and taking his fluids as needed.

The fourth day in the morning, when his parents visited, he looked much brighter, sitting up in bed he greeted them with a cheery smile. 'Hello, Mum and Dad, I feel much better, I can think better and have a clearer head. I feel I can leave hospital and am slowly beginning to remember things from my past, like my trip to the jungles, and fighting the poachers. Maybe if everyone keeps reminding me of past events, I will fully regain my memory. I certainly don't want to think too much about my near miss with death. I must thank the tracker who saved my life,' he said, limping out of bed, with a badly sprained ankle.

'What a miracle! What a miracle!' both John and Gladys said together, and Gladys started to cry. The events of the past few days and weeks had been too much to bear. She hugged her son, and John held their hands from his wheelchair. They just sat in that small room in the hospital, each with their own thoughts, words being redundant at a time such as this. Emotionally and physically exhausted, Gladys wiped her eyes, John blew his nose, and Digby tried to take in the magnitude of all the recent happenings in his life.

'All I can really remember is seeing those terrifying small eyes of that mother elephant charging down at me, and the gun shots ringing in my ears with three elephants dead at my feet,' and he started retching and shaking.

They just sat there, then got into a family huddle of embrace, and needed time, lots of time to process all that had happened. It was horrific and frightening, recalling the events.

Leaving hospital, they decided to spend another day in the

house at Puttalam, Digby now remembering Sunil and Bandara, Palitha and Dhanasiri, and the tracker from his previous visit, who, on this occasion had saved his life. Words were insufficient to thank his tracker.

'Sir, no need to thank me, I was just doing my job.' And what a job to be sure.

•••

John and Gladys had to plan their trip back to Melbourne, but for now this was paradise. Sitting around the lagoon at sunset, watching the sun, burning red, sink into the sea was magical. In the evening, an ardent frenzied life seemed to break out. Countless shelled crabs and other shelled animals begin to crawl about at the edge of the water, and in the water every living thing seemed to move about. Small fish swam in little pools of water, larger fish leapt around, and sometimes large, coloured fish gleamed above the surface. Millions of tiny shrimps swam around, and the occasional lobster could be found amidst deeper rocks. A visual delight to all lovers of sea creatures.

Sitting in the veranda of their bungalow, they marvelled at the lovely evening – there was something magical about it. The night was wonderfully silent. Not a breath of wind in the air, only a delightful balminess. Now and again a night owl gave a mournful cry, and the swaying coconut trees silhouetted against the sky seem to be listening. The half-moon just rising in the sky, and a million stars, filled the clear cloudless sky like tiny fairy lights. Just so beautiful to the human eye; it had to be the work of a celestial being.

•••

The next morning Gladys phoned Zelma, 'We have wonderful news. Digby is almost back to his old self, and we will catch the first available flight back to Australia. John and I have seen so much; but Digby will have much more to tell you when he is ready. He is presently recovering from several mind-boggling events and will have plenty to fill you in with. I'll let you know when we have made plans. It'll be better to give him a few days to rest before he can recall as much as he can.'

'Oh, Gladys, that's such wonderful news. I can't wait to meet you all, especially Digby. I will wait to hear further from you. Maybe I'll pretend to him that I know nothing of this, in case he contacts me to tell me himself,' said an ecstatic Zelma, who was dancing around the room.

I *can't wait to meet him again, to hear his voice, to take up where we left off,* said Zelma to herself, so grateful that things were now improving.

Digby was vaguely aware that Zelma was waiting to hear from him, and wanted to surprise her, rather than give her the news by telephone, telling his parents as much, leaving Gladys caught between a rock and a hard place.

The Trotts spent two blissful and relaxing days in Colombo before boarding a non-stop flight back to Melbourne. Digby was trying to remember Zelma, and all they had, his parents constantly reminding him of his life before his accident. He wasn't quite sure how to approach the subject. Maybe a phone call to her, or no, maybe a visit; he was tossing up as to how he could renew the friendship with her. He certainly was waiting impatiently to meet her again as he tried to envisage how all that would progress.

•••

Flight UL 48 on Saturday was due to touch down in Melbourne at 1640 hours. It was a fully booked flight. Digby had a window seat, and sat quietly gazing out of the plane window, his mind flitting from one scene to another. What a momentous few days it had been. He had met up with Tissa the day before he left Colombo, grateful for all his assistance. The poachers who were caught were all charged and were in prison, but the masterminds behind the racket were still at large. This angered Digby, especially after all he had been through. Sitting there contemplating the poaching racket, he mused that the job was yet unfinished. Tissa had not discussed any further plans to apprehend them, if any. Digby was fully compensated for the time off work and his medical injuries, but he felt the work was unfinished.

What of the future? There was so much to look forward to, and to reflect on the past. It all seemed surreal, almost a dream. Would he wake up to face reality? He pushed those thoughts out of his head and tuned into tranquil music on the plane sound system.

He woke out of his reverie to hear the captain say, 'Prepare for landing, kindly fasten your seat belts and adjust your seats to the upright position.'

The plane landed smoothly, taxing to a stop, which gave him a jolt. Collecting their hand luggage, getting passports checked and collecting their baggage, the family lined up for a taxi to their Melbourne hotel.

EIGHTEEN

HOME AGAIN

It was seven pm when Digby knocked on Zelma's apartment door. She was just finishing her dinner, and in her night attire. The night outside was blowing a gale, the wind howling around the trees, but Zelma was unaware of the weather. Digby was casually dressed in jeans, shirt and sneakers. Zelma opened the door and couldn't believe her eyes. Her old Digby was standing there, looking slightly slimmer, but otherwise back to the man she had gone out with. She invited him in and wasn't sure how she should greet him. After all, the last time they met he couldn't remember her. Would he now?

Digby too, was apprehensive, although he couldn't quite recall how he had reacted to her recently. 'Hello, Zelma,' and he held out his hand to greet her, but she gave him a peck on his cheek.

He went on, 'This is awkward. I understand I didn't treat you too well when I returned after my injury, and I want to offer you my sincere apologies. I feel different now, even though I can't quite remember all that happened, but things are slowly coming back to me.'

'No need to apologise. I'm so glad that you are now recovered. I'll pour us a drink, while you get comfortable on the couch,' Zelma awkwardly replied.

They sat down just looking at each other, as he held her hand. Zelma with tears welling up in her eyes, kept looking at him, repeatedly. She couldn't speak, words seemed redundant.

'It was a nightmare, and I feel I'm now living a dream and hope the nightmare never returns. I've so much ground to cover. Most importantly I must find a job when the doctors tell me I can return to work. There's so much to say,' Digby went on. 'Maybe we should just spend tonight quietly together, and catch up with all the reminiscing another time,' feeling loss of face, and embarrassment at the way he had treated her.

'Yes, I totally agree. Tonight, is for celebrating.' Zelma sounded overjoyed. 'You can stay here for the night if you like, now that you haven't accommodation in the city.'

'Thank you for the kind offer. I know I must get back to Gippsland, and sort out matters there, until I have a job in Melbourne, or maybe I'll find a job in the country. But that will keep us further apart. Rentals here are expensive, I'll have to ask the old man for a loan,' Digby said, half tempted to take up her offer, but he had to let his head rule his heart. He felt they had to re-establish their relationship once more; it was strange the second time around. It almost felt like they were strangers.

Zelma knew she couldn't rush Digby; she had to give him time to come to terms with the situation from where he left off. She didn't even know how much he remembered of her.

He was appraising her intently, knew he was attracted to her, but had to take things slowly and was not yet ready to plunge in at the deep end. Tonight, was not the night to rush things.

'This has been quite a journey for us,' Digby was contemplative. 'I'm so glad you waited for me and supported me, through what I understand was not very flattering behaviour. Let's play some quiet music and dance slowly. May I have this dance with you?'

After about an hour Digby was leaving, telling her that he, with his parents were leaving for Gippsland by train the next morning, John having to travel in a wheelchair.

Zelma told him, 'Please let me drive you all back. It's no trouble.'

'Thank you. I'll speak to them and call you in the morning. I know we have plenty of luggage and dad has his collapsible wheelchair; and it might just be too much for your sedan.' Giving her a kiss goodbye, he set out for his hotel.

He was in a melancholic mood at having left Zelma alone. Much as he wanted to stay, he had to let his mind run free, pick up the pieces of his life and start all over again. How he hated the poachers. His trip hadn't turned out the way he had wanted it to, he reminisced.

•••

Digby phoned Zelma the next morning, 'Zelma, my parents want to travel by train, and don't want to inconvenience you. I'll have to leave with them but I will certainly be in contact sooner rather than later.' John and Gladys with Digby set off by train for Morwell, John breathing a sigh of relief that he and Gladys could now return to their quiet life back on the farm. Arriving in the afternoon they found there had been an unknown infection on the farm, killing several of their sheep, and some of their goats. Moreover, a fox had entered their chicken coop and killed several of their best laying hens. This was a financial loss they didn't need just currently. The locum farmer had done his best to save the remaining farm animals, for which they were grateful. Perhaps their insurance would come to the party, so John hoped.

•••

Digby phoned Scott, 'Mate, I'm finally back home in one piece, including some bumps and bruises. Call over when you can.'

'So glad to hear you again, mate. Yes, I'll call over, maybe this evening after work. Things have gone well here. Your tenant is on a monthly contract, so you can move back in there when ready. I guess you'll want to tee up some work first. Catch you this evening.'

Scott arrived, unsure of what to expect. Would he be the man of old, or an entirely new person?

When Scott arrived, he gave Digby a huge embrace, and they went down to the Morwell Hotel together.

'So good to see you. Looking fine too, I might add. We were all very concerned about you.'

Scott looked him up and down, 'Hmmm, lost a bit of weight, got a healthy tan, and a few grey hairs I imagine, after all you've been through. You'll have to update me on your adventures.'

'Scotty, I wanted so much to remember my recent past life, but I guess I needed a shock of huge proportions to restore it. The actual events with the elephants are vague; I was too terrified to remember much. All I thought of was that I was going to die. I had a near death experience, I guess. My life flashed before my eyes. It was very, very, scary. The work is unfinished. Those masterminds of the poaching gangs are not yet apprehended. My head is still rather foggy, will need a few days to recover, I guess. I'll have to settle down to work here, and maybe recruit some help with catching the poachers. Want to volunteer? Maybe uncle Fred could help. These all seem like pipe dreams of mine!' Digby said in a thoughtful mood.

'I agree, they are ambitious plans. Exotic wildlife is not my scene. Sheep and cattle will do me fine. Settle down to life here before you even think of going back. Besides, I don't think your parents could take any more drama; they are not young anymore, and I'm sure that if you are with Zelma, she wouldn't approve.'

They enjoyed a few beers, had a pub meal, and returned to the Trott farm, so Scott could greet John and Gladys. 'Good to see you, Scott,' Gladys greeted him warmly. John adding, 'We have heaps to tell you. Want to hang around?'

'Not today, John. I must get going. Perhaps it will need mountains of time.'

•••

On Monday, Digby contacted his Melbourne doctor informing him of his progress and apparent cure. His doctor was delighted and had received information from the Puttalam Hospital as to his condition.

He then contacted his previous employer to ask him if there was an available vacancy in the IT Department. Unfortunately, his position had been filled, but they were expanding and there could be a vacancy in a few weeks' time. Not being so happy with the work there, Digby set about looking for alternate positions, deciding to stay in Melbourne. He also needed to rest both mentally and physically. His parents, keen for him to rest at home with them, now bonded closer than ever to their son.

He needed to check out his Mirboo North holiday house sometime; perhaps Scott would drive him down. Scott and Digby planned to set out on the weekend to check on his house and thank the neighbours. He also had to reconnect with Zelma. On the following weekend, Scott arrived to oversee Digby's driving on the long winding country roads to Mirboo, hoping to help Digby regain some confidence. A half hour drive from Morwell to Mirboo took them to Digby's cottage. The garden was unmaintained, a careless tenant strewing empty beer cans in the unkempt garden. The inside was messy and needed a good clean. The agent had to be told off, politely. Digby wanted to give his tenant notice to vacate but did need the rent to help pay off his mortgage. Perhaps when he secured work again, he would reclaim his property; the thoughts swirling in his mind.

The two of them then drove to the Traralgon airport and inspected the airport tower; now restored and renovated. Jack was not a suspect in the eyes of the investigating officer, even though arson was mildly suspected. It was deemed an accidental fire from a malfunctioning heater. Crop dusting work was slow, not being the season for it, obviously good news for Digby.

'Let's visit Jack and drop in on him unannounced,' Scott suggested to which Digby enthusiastically agreed. Driving past Jack's house in nearby Morwell they found him lazing on a veranda couch, asleep in the early afternoon, with a few empty beer stubbies around him. Scott beeped his horn, to which Jack jumped up with a start.

'Strewth, what the hell are you blaring your horn for?' he hollered, clearly annoyed that his siesta had been interrupted.

Walking up to the car he noticed his mates and beamed, 'Digby, Scott, haven't seen you guys in ages. Come on in.'

They sauntered into a very untidy house, full of clothes, shoes, stale food and cardboard takeaway boxes strewn all over the floor, in a lounge room full of the smell of staleness. Mice and possum droppings were on the floor and in the yard. All they could do was walk out into fresh air and not be nauseated.

'Jack, this place is most unhealthy. You need to give it a good clean,' Scott hollered at him.

'I've been busy working and couldn't find the time. Besides, I do take exemption to your dropping in unannounced,' Jack retorted. He had a point there, they silently acknowledged.

Trying to get him to join them for a coffee, he declined.

'Been working five days a week, which is better than I was doing a year ago. Not in tow with too many of my old mates, and even found a girlfriend!'

'Really,' they both said in unison. 'Now, that's very good news. What's she like?' Digby asked.

To which Jack just smiled, and appeared very mysterious. 'I'll let you know in good time.'

Maybe his Aunt Betty could fill in the missing information. Waving goodbye to Jack they drove past Betty's house, only to find her out.

•••

The two of them then drove back to the farm where Digby was keen to regale Scott of his adventures, at least of those he could recall. Scott wasn't too sure it would have been an accurate description, but nevertheless was keen to hear his story.

'I knew I was a real thorn in people's sides, an upstart and an idiot in so many ways. Took unnecessary risks, unaware of danger, and never learnt from my mistakes, which almost cost me my life. Rather like Jack when we first knew him. Glad that my parents were around to keep an eye on things. That is one part of my life I'd like to forget.'

As Digby didn't want to recount his past bad behaviour Scott went along with that, as he already knew enough about it.

'Anyway, I really would like to finish that business of apprehending the poacher master- minds, if that would be possible. I wonder if it would come to pass?'

•••

He had some unfinished business with his treating doctor in Melbourne and scheduled an early appointment with him. The doctor welcomed him into his consulting room. 'Hello, Digby, come in and have a seat. I see that you are feeling much better now. I will run a few tests on you and then have our resident neuropsychologist see you to determine your fitness to work. How do you feel in yourself? Do you feel ready to return to work?'

'Yes, doc. If you tell me, I have passed all my tests, then perhaps, I'll feel confident regarding returning to work.'

All tests being successful Digby met up with Zelma. He had to find work and a place to live, reasoning he'd take boarding-house digs and find work in the first instance.

Making several applications for work he was called up for a few interviews and was fortunate to land a job with a large IT company.

He drove down to Melbourne for a weekend stay. Looking for and securing accommodation, he arrived for dinner at Zelma's place where they sat down for a cosy chat by the fireplace. It was winter and that meant snow in the highlands. Although he hadn't skied before, he was a quick learner, and knew that Zelma was also a skier.

After being in his new job for a couple of weeks they talked about doing a day trip to a snowfield within driving distance from Melbourne.

They were reigniting their love, which was especially romantic when the days were getting shorter and the nights longer and cosier. He had settled into work and had a bit more disposable income, so went out for dinner at a restaurant in Williamstown by the sea. The sea was angry, the waves breaking loudly on the shore and a choppiness in the deep waters not seen in summer. The sky was overcast, the clouds pregnant with rain, and with the darkness of night, the rain began to fall, a light drizzle that hovered over the land like a fine mist, as darkness fell.

'It is so great that we can be together again, after all you have been through.' Zelma was wistful and sentimental, almost tearful, as she reminisced on the recent past.

Digby just squeezed her hand, looked into her eyes, and said nothing for a while.

'I was very fortunate that I had you by my side throughout; you were my rock.'

'I would do it all over again, my darling,' Zelma said in a quiet and contemplative mood. Little needed to be said, there was an intense feeling of togetherness.

•••

Having finished their delicious meal, washed down with wine, they walked on the boardwalk, and left to head back to her apartment. Cuddling up on the couch, listening to soft music, they were relaxed, and loved up, so they gently moved onto her queen-sized bed. In no time they were back to where they left off on that hot night in Puttalam. It had been quite a while, they needed to find their love again, and they both climaxed simultaneously. Lying together in each other's arms they fell asleep to dream of things to come.

•••

Deciding to drive down to Digby's weekender on Saturday they set off early. Coming into Korumburra, snow was beginning to fall. It was so beautiful, the tiny snowflakes like bits of cotton wool coming down from the heavens. It must have been decades since there was snow in Gippsland.

'My goodness, what a beautiful sight!' Digby was ecstatic. 'I will have to drive really slow; the road is treacherous.'

Zelma added, 'This is a winter wonderland. Let's get out and enjoy it with those young boys throwing snowballs.' They did just that, laughing and falling in the snow.

They arrived at Mirboo North to sit on the deck and watch the ground and the nearby fields become completely covered in a thin blanket of snow. On the roads young boys were tobogganing down the grass covered snow on the median strips.

'This is amazing, I've never seen such a spectacle in all the years I've lived here,' Digby exclaimed, grabbing his camera. They put on warm and waterproof gear and walked out into the snow just allowing it to fall all over them. Snowball throwing was on the agenda, delighting in laughter and happiness, aiming the white stuff at each other.

They were like little kids again, enjoying a rare and wonderful morning.

NINETEEN

DRAMA ON THE SNOW-COVERED ROAD

Waking on Sunday morning, and sitting on the deck drinking tea, they decided to take a day trip to the Victorian snow fields. It had to be Lake Mountain; for Digby it was his first experience of thick snow, for Zelma an experience she loved. Digby was always won over by heat and farm animals, but snow was something new to him. Getting into Digby's car they left early after a quick breakfast. Marysville for a stopover was on the cards. It was a rainy winter's day and snow predicted on the snowfields. They rugged up with the warmest clothes they owned, boots included. Digby was advised to get snow chains for his tyres and drive cautiously, setting off with sandwiches and hot chocolate in a flask. There was a slow drizzle of rain they drove into, an uphill climb in low gear. Not owning an all-wheel drive Digby had to be extra cautious. At about ten thirty they stopped for coffee at a small café in Marysville. After a good leg stretch, they climbed back into their car to continue to the top of the mountain. It was a winding wet road and fog lights were necessary. Going round a bend they met a car on the wrong side of the road coming headlong onto them.

Digby shouted, 'My God, what's that man doing?' he screamed.

The next thing they knew their car was hurtling down the side of the road, down a sheer precipice and going downhill. They both had their seat belts on and were tossed around, the car landing on its wheels.

She looked up. There were trees everywhere; she tried to grab the steering wheel crying out, 'Digby, what's happening?' The car ended up against a tree, the windscreen shattered, saw him slumped across the steering wheel, head down. Something thumped into her chest – the air bag – she was trying to draw air into her lungs. A smell of burning oil and black smoke filled the car; the seat belt tightening across her chest. She closed her eyes and slowly drifted into oblivion.

Quick as a flash some onlookers were down the hill to drag them out of the wreck – the car now severely damaged. A fire engine and tow truck were on the scene within minutes. An ambulance with sirens blazing arrived, to transport them to a hospital in Melbourne.

Just as they were picking up the pieces of their lives, along comes another setback. The seat belts had saved their lives.

She was muttering in her semi-conscious state, 'Digby help me, I'm in pain.'

A case of deja vu for him, his body and mind getting more than a fair share of knocks. Arriving at the hospital, they were immediately wheeled into the intensive care unit for close monitoring.

Both Digby's and Zelma's parents arrived at the hospital in no time, keeping a vigil at their bedsides. Back to tests for Digby, his body was certainly getting a workover. Being in separate wards they couldn't check on each other, getting news via their parents.

'I certainly feel more mobile using this wheelie walker,' John confided to Gladys.

Another hospital stay for Digby, and this time Zelma as well. Zelma had an extra complication of bleeding, and it was determined she had miscarried. She had no idea she was pregnant, as she had not missed a period; but having irregular periods she didn't know she was pregnant. She was rather glad it turned out that way, as a pregnancy was not something she could have dealt with… there was far too much going on in her life already.

Out of intensive care Digby was delighted to hear that Zelma was improving.

Digby was discharged after a few days in hospital, but Zelma had to stay in longer, for a week all up. The body aches and pains a constant reminder of how fortunate they were; both thanked their lucky stars it had turned out that way.

When Zelma was discharged from the ward, she needed some rehabilitation and breathing exercises, needing another week in hospital. Finally, she left the sterile environment for home in her apartment. That night Digby picked up some dinner and they ate at Zelma's place.

'This could have been so much worse. What was that man thinking coming into my side of the road. Roads on hill climbs are always treacherous. I think somebody up there was looking after us, my love.'

'I agree. What a horrible experience. Never again, if I can help it.'

He was able to recommence his work with his new employer soon afterwards, his car replaced by his insurance company. They both decided this was their karma. they were meant to be together.

•••

Digby phoned Tissa, 'How are things progressing in sunny Sri Lanka, Tissa?'

'Well, the poachers in custody are a rowdy lot, but refusing to give us any information; I'll need to try more severe methods to make them talk. I'm working on it.'

'Keep me posted, please. I'll try and think up some ideas. Maybe Fred might be worth getting in on the scene.'

•••

Digby was able to rent a two-bedroom apartment with borrowed basic furniture near his newly found job, and they went on frequent trips to his cottage, Zelma acquiring a new-found appreciation for country life. Tissa updated him on how the court case brought by the police against the poachers was progressing, which was very slow, and to support him in tracking down the masterminds behind the corrupt racket.

It was in one such e-mail that Tissa mentioned the difficulty the Wildlife Department was faring in finding the gang leaders.

He hit on an idea to enlist his Uncle Fred, who lived in Sri Lanka, as to whether he had any ideas on how they could be apprehended.

Fred wrote back, 'Digby, my boy, these are hardened criminals. They know the jungle very well. I feel I know the jungle well too, but they must have a gang of them; it's big business for them.'

'I'd like to wreak vengeance on them. They set up their henchmen to try and destroy me. Why don't we get together with Tissa to formulate a plan to apprehend them, perhaps in the Yala Game Park in Block three?' was Digby's response.

'That sounds good in theory. Let me make some enquiries at this end and try to determine their modus operandi, their habitats, and any other information I can collect. It will be advantageous if we had access to a helicopter, or failing that, a drone to determine their movements, but I guess the funds wouldn't stretch that far. Local communities, and villagers in the area may be able to help, if they can be depended upon to keep the investigations private and secret; rather doubtful, I'm afraid. Let me know your thoughts as well as Tissa's,' Fred emailed Digby.

Digby phoned Tissa to get his input. 'Tissa, you have read Fred's comments. The helicopter, and/or a drone may be impossible, but it is a good idea.'

'I will investigate it. I think a drone is a possibility; that way we could determine their hideouts, and target those areas, instead of going in blind. The court cases in this country take months, sometimes years to get to their allocated timeline, so it will be a while before we get anywhere. Catching the masterminds may be possible before then. The captured poachers will not divulge any information. I also investigated your idea that there may be a spy from the poaching gang in the town. That could be possible. I'll try and investigate the idea although it's not easy as it is difficult to get the trust of the villagers.'

Digby took all this information on board and decided Fred would be a useful ally; he would let him investigate matters before he decided to make another trip overseas; it was too soon after commencing his new job. Apprehending the masterminds could not be done in a hurry.

•••

Digby and Zelma had a quiet dinner at his apartment. He was

enjoying his new job, and wanted to discuss it with her, and she was trying to instill in him some housekeeping and tidiness. After a beautifully cooked roast dinner he wanted to bring her up to date with his progress in trying to apprehend the criminal syndicate in the jungles.

'Zelma, my sweet, I am in contact with my mother's brother Fred, who I went on a safari with a few years ago, hunting the man-eater of a leopard killer in Vakarani. Well, I've asked him to assist Tissa and the others including myself, to apprehend the mastermind criminals in Yala, and he will do some preliminary investigations.'

'Don't tell me you're thinking of going back there again after all you have been through? That's most foolhardy of you, Digby Trott! You must have rocks in your head. Let Tissa find the masterminds. Why do you have to go into that death trap to locate them?'

'Not now, my love. He will gather as much information as he can and join the team if we are going to take up the challenge again. He is a master hunter, and a real asset to the team. The masterminds must be brought to justice.'

'I really hope you know what you are getting into. It must be very certain this time if you are going to make another trip. What about your job here? I doubt new employers will be lenient with granting leave.'

Digby didn't want to upset Zelma too much, deciding to let the conversation end. He would like her to accompany him when he made the next trip, albeit a short one, so he hoped. He noticed she was getting another panic attack, her breathing becoming more rapid, and she was starting to retch. No good upsetting her, he thought. *Each time I bring up a controversial subject she gets nervous.*

•••

Scott contacted Digby to determine how his new job was progressing, hoping to meet him at his weekender in Mirboo North.

'Digby, if you are down in this neck of the woods, there is crop dusting to be done this weekend. Why not get together after work on Saturday?'

That weekend Zelma was off to her parents' home and Digby drove to South Gippsland for work and socialising. After work Scott and he went down to the pub and ran into Jack who was with a couple of his mates. He was rather sober, they were pleased to notice. He joined them.

'How's the new job going?' Scott asked Digby.

'Fairly routine stuff. I've been there three months now and I reckon the company is keen to make me permanent. Must keep my options open, though; see if I can find something rather more challenging. Scotty, how would you like to join me and maybe Zelma and my Uncle Fred in Sri Lanka to apprehend the poacher masterminds? Hopefully, it will be a short trip, as Fred is doing all the preliminary investigations in collaboration with Tissa, right now.'

'I'll have to give it some thought, as wildlife and jungles are not my scene. However, the thrill and excitement of the trip might just sway me. Please, keep me in the loop, especially if Fred makes good progress with his investigations.'

Jack was taking in all the developments of the conversation but didn't want to barge in to talk about himself. He was now improving rapidly on the social front.

After their meal, the threesome went their separate ways, Digby to his weekender to clear the garden, now quite overgrown. He had a chat with the neighbours, always a good idea in the rural environment, as each one looks out for the other.

Returning to Melbourne, he and Zelma met on Sunday night for a cosy chat and dinner, Digby careful not to bring up any conversation about returning to apprehend the criminal masterminds, talking about his new job instead. Zelma however had other ideas.

'I will come with you this time, Digby. I don't want you to go into this mad idea of a trip alone. You could be killed and was extremely lucky the last time; your luck may have run out, who knows.'

'I'm aware of all the risks, my sweet. With you at my side I'll feel safer, not alone.'

'Is that pressure on me to come along? You're such a charmer. I feel my arm is being twisted.'

TWENTY

FRED ASSISTS THE TEAM

Fred set about visiting Yala surrounds to get to know the locals. He was reasonably fluent in Sinhala and tried to determine if any bush meat was sold in their village.

'Where does this meat come from?' he asked at the local market.

'The mudalali man who lives in the big house brings it here every weekend.'

Not certain if the mudalali was one of the masterminds, Fred had to be careful as to how he approached him. He went down to the meat market during the week and observed the vendors, and who they mingled with, but that didn't give him any concrete information to act upon. He befriended one of the vendors.

'Machang, where does this meat come from?' he asked the vendor.

'Mahataya (master), there is a boutique at the next bend of the road, and we collect it from there. I'm told it comes from the jungle at night. Why do you ask?'

'Just curious to know, as there seems to be plenty of meat. Who kills the animals?'

'That, I don't know. I'm just a poor man trying to earn a living from selling meat for the mudalali,' declared the vendor. He was dressed in a sarong tied at his waist, and a tank top, and he had betel stains on his teeth from chewing betel. He was barefoot and lean, displaying his bones; typical of all the market vendors.

Fred decided he was not going to obtain any more information at the markets and moved on.

On the weekend Fred arrived at the market to observe the rich mudalali, who was seen with gold rings on his fingers, and a thick gold chain around his neck, fat and opulent looking, he wore an exotic sarong held up at the waist by a belt, a white clean long-sleeved shirt, with fancy sandals on his feet, smoking a cigar. He had to be up to some racket, so Fred surmised.

Sitting in proximity of his conversation, he overheard him telling one of the vendors that there had been a large haul of meat recently and they could expect a good supply, for the next town as well.

Travelling to the next small village Fred drove around trying to locate the movements of the locals, who were getting increasingly suspicious of the 'white man' who had arrived in their town, for no apparent reason.

Maybe he needed to do a trip into the Yala Park and survey the area from the inside, his next plan.

As usual he needed a tracker and a four-wheel drive vehicle to enter the park, doing so very early at about six am when the animals were just out looking for food, to try and detect any unusual movements from humans. Going straight into Block three, he noticed three men walking about among the tall bushes, for no apparent reason. Keeping hidden as far as he could, together with the tracker, and the driver they followed the men in their vehicle. The men were setting up fences made from thorny bushes in as straight a line as possible. Every few hundred metres there was a gap in the fence through which animals could pass. These gaps were snared with wire traps to catch and torture wild animals. Fred could not apprehend the poachers, but he now knew their modus operandi. Going on a little further he noticed at the edge of the jungle a clearing, and a small mud hut. In the clearing there were strapped to the ground, five spotted deer skins, held down with makeshift strong pointed sticks. This was clearly where the men brought their dead animals. At that time of day, early in the morning, there were no men around the mud hut; Fred was ecstatic that he had found this lair. Tissa now had some concrete evidence to go on and Digby would be pleased. Perhaps drones may be able to take some pictures of all the discoveries.

•••

'Tissa, could you send a surveillance drone to survey the jungle in Yala Park Block three? There is a small camp there which I'm sure the poachers and their leaders use for cleaning the dead animals. If we can catch them in the act, we'll have caught our criminals.'

Tissa set about organising a drone to survey the jungle and around the mudalali's residence. He came back with photographs of the poachers from the jungle, and presumably the mudalali in the adjoining village, which needed further investigation.

Fred phoned Digby, 'I have some useful investigation on the poaching syndicate. There is a flourishing camp site going on in Block three, which Tissa will investigate. If you are planning to return and confront them it may be a good idea to organise your time off work, and for time off for anyone else you want to bring with you.'

Digby became very interested. It was a few months since he had started his new job, and he wasn't sure how his employer would respond to his application for leave. Zelma too, felt uncertain about taking any more leave to travel overseas. Scott, if he intended joining them, felt it would be alright organising time off his work.

Digby approached his employer, 'I know I haven't been working here too long; there is an opportunity for me to join a safari group led by my uncle, a superb marksman to apprehend poachers, who I bear a vendetta against, and capture their leaders. I wonder if I could be granted some leave maybe for two weeks?" he asked in trepidation.

'Of course, my dear man, that is a once in a life-time experience, you must go,' his employer responded.

A relieved and surprised Digby was thrilled with his reply.

He phoned Zelma, 'Guess what? My boss is encouraging me to go on the safari. I'm taking two weeks off work. Hope you are as fortunate as that.'

Zelma wasn't certain she would be granted leave but was determined not to let Digby travel alone this time. He'd had more than his fair share of knocks and injury. Scott was joining them as well and had his leave approved.

Plans could now be made for all-out war with the poachers, led by Fred.

Tissa was contacted, and he suggested Dhanasiri, Sunil and Bandara join as well if required.

Once flights were organised, they planned to travel direct to the bungalow in Buttala, deciding there was no need for a stay in Colombo. As usual John and Gladys would keep an eye on his flat in Melbourne and his house in Mirboo, but not before John had made his disapproval known, and he was very vocal about Digby making yet another trip to catch poachers.

'When are you going to learn? Haven't you had enough of fighting this "war" with criminals?' he roared at his son when he heard the news. 'Fred may be a good marksman, but you are risking your life, and I'm not yet convinced that there is anything to be gained from this. Call it vengeance if you like. I call it stupidity.'

Digby too excited to take in what his father said. He ignored the comment.

John went on, 'Don't expect your mother and me to come after you. We are too old for these adventures now. I hope you know what you're doing.'

•••

The three of them packed their bags for yet another trip to the subcontinent, Zelma quite nervous as to what this trip envisaged. Fred's shooting skills noted, she was convinced it was dangerous, nevertheless. She had another panic attack when buying her ticket with Digby by her side. He was accustomed to her nervousness and tried to calm her down, as Lucy had instructed him to ensure she always had a squeeze ball with her and a brown paper bag in her handbag. On departure day they took a taxi to the airport, with minimal luggage, with Digby carrying a rifle as well.

As usual the direct flight from Melbourne touched down at Colombo's International Airport at about midnight with Digby, Zelma and Scott on board, Zelma fared better with Digby at her side; mild aviophobia and some increased rapid breathing, now well controlled, to her delight. They were booked into an Airport Hotel for the night. Dhanasiri, and Fred, arrived the next morning to drive them to the house in Buttala, which was going to be their base for the trip. No other towns on the island had been scheduled for stopovers.

As it was Scott's first trip to Sri Lanka, they made it a slow journey, stopping along the way at various places, to let Scott soak in the culture – Sunil and Bandara were already in residence and waiting for them, arriving at their home from home.

'This is surreal and tranquil,' Scott enthused. 'Hope I can tolerate the food.' Not having been introduced to eastern food, he had brought along all necessary 'upset tummy' medications. 'The sounds of the jungle, call of the wild, I guess that's what it's called, will make up for any other short comings.'

He sat in the garden in the cool of the evening, listening to bird calls, chik chaks on the walls, watching the sun set over a large water tank, all exhilarating to his senses.

•••

After a night's rest, Digby and Fred got together to work out their plan of action. Fred had his high-powered rifle, and Digby was allowed to bring his rifle into Sri Lanka, both very necessary on their mission. It was planned that only Digby, Fred, Sunil, Bandara and Dhanasiri would leave in two days' time for the entrance to the Yala Game Park after collecting the necessary tracker.

Fred went on, 'As foot safaris are permitted in Block three, we will leave our vehicle with Dhanasiri in it, and the five of us will proceed as quietly as possible to within earshot of the clearing I found where animal carcasses are being stored. It is thick jungle, and visibility is not the best, but if the weather gods smile on us, we will be able to see the criminals. I'm sure the mudalali and his men will be there; he must be the leader of the poachers. When the time is right, I will go in announcing our intent and charging him with poaching. My language is adequate for him to understand me. Digby, the other three and you will follow in single file. If he denies my accusations and starts shooting, you and I will open fire. Don't shoot until he fires the first shot. Got the plan?'

'What about Sunil, Bandara and the tracker? What role will they play?' Digby asked.

'They will be the back-up crew, for fisticuffs, and to support us. If no guns are fired, then we will have to fight man-to-man to the end. But I'm almost sure there will be a gun battle.'

'All understood. We must bring the others into the picture; tell them our plan,' Digby said, shifting around in his chair. 'You know this jungle; I'm there with you all the way. This is going to be exhilarating, and fraught with danger, no doubt about that.'

Digby had to speak to Zelma. 'My love, Fred and I and the rest of us are leaving tomorrow morning except for Scott and you, to go into Block three. We will most likely be back in the afternoon. We plan to apprehend the poaching masterminds.'

Zelma sat there stony-faced, trying hard to avert yet another panic attack. She realised the danger they were getting into; voicing her fears to Digby, she realised, was futile; his mind set was stubborn and unshakeable.

•••

The men awoke early the next day, and after breakfast, set out as planned to enter the main gate, collect the tracker, and proceed through Blocks one and two into the desolate and overgrown jungle that is Block three. There was a river running through the middle of the jungle with thick bushes and evergreen trees in abundance. Animals roamed freely as there was no tourist traffic. Bird sounds, deer barking, leopard sawing, elephant trumpeting, all in a day's excitement; together with criminal activity.

Driving silently, they proceeded slowly towards the area that Fred had located, and ear- marked, there being only silence and jungle sounds to greet them. Coming within vicinity of the campsite they parked and left Dhanasiri in the vehicle. Thick bushes and trees all around, as they alighted from the vehicle, they formed a single line with Fred leading, the other three in between and Digby at the rear. They moved quietly, taking care not to tread on sticks or dry twigs. Coming closer they saw through the trees, five men slaughtering a deer with the mudalali and another man looking on, presumably another boss. They silently watched for a good half an hour, waiting for the right time to rush in on them.

Fred led the way quietly into the compound. 'What are these animal skins doing on the ground?'

'None of your business, and who are you all anyway? We are not harming anybody. You have no authority to come here, barging in on our work,' the mudalali responded.

Two of the poachers started attacking Sunil and Bandara, and a fight broke out. Arms and legs swinging, flying into others faces, the poachers, breathing heavily, seeming to be professional boxers as well, hit out heavily. Digby went to their rescue, his pulse racing, sweat pouring from his brow, and getting very agitated, trying to use his karate skills, but not contacting anyone. Memories of the past came surging forth, and the mudalali pulled out a gun; Digby, noticing this, used his long leg in a karate swing and knocked the gun out of his hand just as he fired a shot. Fred quick on the draw and with a determined stare, shot the mudalali in the torso, bringing him down. Digby rushed to Fred's aid and shot two of the poachers in their chests, snap, crack, bang, whilst he ducked and hid behind a large bush, desperation at his forefront, this was one battle he wouldn't allow the poachers to get a hold on. Only two of the adversaries carried guns, which helped the team get in with advantage. Fred was shouting to his men to capture the criminals, 'Get a hold of them, hand cuff them, don't let them get away.'

The mudalali was writhing in pain, his assistant, his arm and chest bleeding from gunshot wounds, fell to the ground and one of Digby's team arrested him. Digby was breathing heavily, malice and retribution at the fore front of his mind. He hated them immensely, every sinew of his muscles telling him to wreak vengeance. In a few minutes all was silent, the mudalali and his assistant shot and on the ground. Fred shot in the left arm and shoulder was bleeding, three other poachers all handcuffed by Digby and his men.

Looking at the scene Digby felt an immense sense of relief, that the mastermind had been captured, his life endangered as he was bleeding profusely, probably a main artery had been lacerated. His chief assistant lay gasping for air as he had been shot in the chest.

Digby went to Fred's side, and with a large piece of cloth torn off his shirt, tied his arm above the bleeding vessel. Fred was drifting off to sleep, and Digby phoned Dhanasiri to bring the vehicle and transport Fred to hospital. The others were handcuffed or lying on the ground, the two main criminals badly injured, but they would have to wait for medical assistance. The deer being slaughtered lay bleeding on the ground, and soon fell on its side, it was too late to save the animal.

•••

Tissa came in at about this time to survey the damage and organised for the poachers to be duly dealt with. 'I can see now how organised this criminal gang is. It has taken us years to find the culprits, and getting Fred in on the job has helped us enormously. I do hope he is not too badly injured and will recover. As for the two ring leaders, they are in a bad way regarding their health. Let's see how they recover, if indeed they do.'

Fred was rushed to the nearest hospital, Dhanasiri doing the driving. Tissa's vehicle transported the others to another hospital and were placed under police guard. At the local hospital Fred underwent emergency surgery to repair the damage to his arm and shoulder. It was touch and go for a few days, with Digby sitting by his side extremely worried. The mudalali succumbed to his injuries, and two of the poachers as well passed away. The next in charge to the boss was under police guard in hospital, and he was to be charged if he fully recovered. Digby and the others in his team managed to survive the ordeal with minor injuries.

Digby returned to the Buttala bungalow to be greeted by Zelma and Scott, tired, battle- weary and on an adrenaline high. The job had been done; now that the ringleader hadn't survived, and his off sider seriously injured. Better to have him alive, is what Tissa reasoned, that way he could be charged and face imprisonment.

Fred's condition hung in the balance for a few days. Tissa and Digby keeping a bed side vigil. But he was a tough jungle warrior and pulled through much to Digby's relief.

● ● ●

Scott was keen to see some of the sights of wild Sri Lanka, and Digby volunteered to be his guide, so, for the next few days the three of them visited the parks that Digby had known so well, giving him happiness and a sense of fulfillment.

Scott hired a driver and vehicle to travel around and into the parks. 'I reckon we can meet some of the locals before going into the parks. I'd like to understand their way of life.'

The driver took them to his relatives' simple mud brick house with a single bedroom and another general-purpose room where a family of four lived. The toilet was a pit toilet outside the house, the water for all purposes coming from a deep well in their back yard. The man was a tree climber who climbed coconut trees for picking coconuts on large estates, earning a meagre income trying to support his family; yet they insisted on inviting the visitors in for a rice and curry meal, which they found hard to refuse.

'Are you happy here?' Scott asked the man, the driver acting as interpreter.

'What can I do, sir? There is no other work for me. At least I can go out to pick coconuts every day. There are some people who don't even have that sort of income,' he replied.

Scott and Digby rewarded them with a generous tip; this being an eye-opener to the three visitors as to how the poor must struggle to survive.

●●●

Driving out of town there was a snake charmer with five cobras by the road, providing a show for tourists, which they stopped to watch. He was blowing a flute and moving his head from side to side whilst the cobras sitting neatly in their wicker baskets, irritated and erect, swayed as if in tune to the music. The snake charmer had the tip of his left index finger missing, no doubt having been stung by some snake or other, as cobra stings are usually fatal unless the fangs and poison glands had been removed. The three visitors watched in fascination; Digby having seen a similar act when a child.

From there they moved on to the surf beach of Arugum Bay.

'I'd like to indulge in a bit of surfing, and meet the local surfers,'

Scott declared as they settled in for a couple of days of sun and surf. After travelling around for another few days, it was time to return to the airport and back to Melbourne.

Digby had to check up on Fred before he left. He was recovering well, and Tissa was going to organise care for him, until he was fully recovered. The two masterminds of the poaching gangs both succumbed to their injuries and Tissa hoped that would see the end of the poachers.

'This is going to be memorable, returning on a plane with Digby next to me now. No more distress and panic, I hope,' a relaxed Zelma announced at the airport, holding Digby's hand.

The flight home was far better than her first outbound flight, and she sent Lucy a message confirming this.

•••

Two weeks later:

They were both together at Zelma's apartment, having a quiet dinner. Digby went out to his car and collected twelve red roses and a bottle of champagne. Sitting on the couch, he put his arm around Zelma, then went down on one knee, holding the magnificent bouquet in his hands, and said,

'My darling will you marry me?'

Zelma was ecstatic and surprised, but very happy that he would ask her after such a short time together, and was blown away with his romantic offering, and knew that he was the one for her; they were meant to be together.

With an almighty, 'Yes, my love, I certainly will,' she returned his embrace.

'We must go out and choose an engagement ring,' Digby said

on cloud nine, 'and share the good news with everyone. We can fix the wedding date for perhaps our next summer, and honeymoon in gorgeous and beautiful Sri Lanka. I'm absolutely over the moon, and it can't happen soon enough. A small wedding perhaps and an extravagant honeymoon. We have so much to save up for,' said a delighted Digby as they sat quietly in each other's arms.

'We have been together for only a short while but have experienced a lifetime of adventure. I have the perfect bottle of champagne. Let's pop the cork. Here's to our future.'

Virginia de Vos is a retired psychiatric medical practitioner, who was born in Sri Lanka, and migrated to Melbourne Australia when in her twenties, after graduating in Colombo. Having often visited the wildlife parks of Sri Lanka with her husband, she learnt to enjoy wild animal behaviour, and the beauty of the Sri Lankan countryside.

She also had a love of writing since her childhood, and after her medical career, has used her intimate knowledge of the culture and people of Sri Lanka to describe a fictional story involving conservation of elephants, and the real-life struggles involved.

She lives in Melbourne Australia.